THE MAN
CALLED BUDD

A PRATT DEMPCY & COMPANY
WESTERN ADVENTURE – BOOK 2

INSPIRED BY TRUE EVENTS

ORRIS SLADE

Cover Illustration by Tamara Schmidt

Contents

Prologue

Near Black Lake, California
March 1880

Budd Mansfield stared down the barrel of a lever-action rifle. The muzzle brushed his nose. He looked into the eyes of his captor without flinching.

A fire crackled nearby as the cool forest air kissed the sweat-dampened skin on the back of his neck. Footfalls circled the fire, bringing his attention to the second man for a brief moment.

The ropes that secured Budd's arms behind his back dug painfully into the flesh of his wrists, but he never struggled against his binds. Two pairs of dark eyes glared down at him. "Why were you followin' us?" snarled the first man as he cocked the rifle.

"I'm here for the girl," Budd replied. He searched around the small camp, peering into the darkness just beyond the amber light cast by the flames. His gaze landed upon Miss Savannah Mills, where she was hogtied and gagged. The poor maid whimpered behind the bandana tied between her teeth. "And I fully intend to walk away with her in hand."

The outlaws cackled.

"You hearin' this, Merl?"

Merl shouted, "Sweet girl ain't goin' nowhere with you!"

The moment the rifle swayed past his head, Budd pulled a hidden blade from his belt and severed the ropes. He sprang forward, bashed his elbow into Dale Murphy's nose, and yanked the firearm from his trembling hands. The laughter stopped immediately. Merl Murphy drew his revolver and aimed at Budd.

Budd shot the gun out of his hand, and Merl raised his arms toward the sky. "I knew you two fools would catch on that I was following you and take me in my sleep like a bunch of cowards," Budd snarled. "And I knew getting caught would lead me to the girl."

"Y-you wanted us to capture you?" Dale stammered in return.

Budd simply nodded sharply and kicked the bottom of Dale's boot. "Tie your cousin up with the ropes. Make it tight."

Dale stumbled as he hurried over to Merl. Budd watched closely as he bound his cousin's arms behind his back. When he was sure the ropes were tight enough, Budd tied up Dale before freeing Miss Mills.

She wrapped her arms around him the second she was free. "Thank you!"

Budd blushed profusely and untangled himself from her grasp. "You are very welcome. Now, are there more of them?"

Miss Mills pointed to a spot in the trees where a faint sliver of light poked through the darkness. "Three more at that camp." She sniffled.

Budd left Miss Mills with Merl Murphy's revolver and pushed on toward the second camp. He moved swiftly through the underbrush, silent in ways no man his size had ever managed.

The outlaws came into sight. Budd shot the first man. He spun with the force of the bullet and dropped to the dirt.

Another outlaw rushed Budd but got knocked back by a shot to his middle. Only the leader remained.

"Surrender," Budd ordered.

The gang leader smiled as he dropped his sidearm on the ground. "I was expecting Sheriff Dawson."

"I owed him a favor," Budd answered. He lowered the rifle just long enough to restrain the leader.

"Then you must be the one they talk about. Budd Mansfield," snorted the outlaw. "The man who hunts criminals but has no interest in money or a badge."

"And you are?"

"Red Murphy."

Budd recognized the name from the wanted posters. He rolled his eyes at the mere mention of the name Murphy these days. The Murphy family was like cockroaches. They were nothing more than petty thieves and scavengers. Kidnapping was unusual for them, though. "Who wanted the girl?"

"Carson Hillard," Red said. "Some fat cat from New York who visited the house she works in. Guess he took a liking to her and thought she should join him in the city."

"And you lot will do anything to line your pockets. No matter how distasteful." Budd led his prisoner back to the others.

He loaded the outlaws onto their horses one by one before he tied the reins to the saddles. Once everyone was secured, the journey back to Sacramento began.

"Mr. Mansfield, I—well, I am grateful for all you've done for me," Miss Mills stated as they finally broke through the tree line.

There was nothing but flat desert between the forest surrounding the town of Black Lake and Sacramento. And Budd knew what the minor hitch in her voice meant. Last thing he wanted was some damsel mooning over him.

"Don't be grateful for what I've done, Miss Mills," he retorted. "Thank Sheriff Dawson. He was the one who wanted you found. I was merely the tool he used to get the job done."

And with that, they carried on to the city in utter silence. Only the sound of hooves pounding against the road broke through the quiet. Dawn slowly peered out over the horizon, lighting their way along the winding paths that cut across the landscape. Sacramento appeared just beyond a few spattering of trees.

Sheriff Dawson waited with his deputies at the edge of town.

"The Murphy cousins," Budd scoffed.

Sheriff Dawson shook his head in disgust. "I should have known. I got half a mind to send them to Reno to work in the labor yard." The lawman paced angrily as his men yanked the outlaws from the backs of their horses. "Make sure they don't escape the cells this time! We don't need this town thinking we're incompetent fools."

Budd lowered himself from the saddle and reached up for Miss Mills.

She avoided his gaze as he helped her down. When her feet touched the ground, she said, "Thank you, Mr. Mansfield. I don't care what you say about the matter… few folks would risk their lives to save a maid."

Chapter 1

Sacramento, California
April 1880

Budd awakened to a frantic knock at his door. He blinked sleep-crusted eyes and let out a throaty groan.

His friend, and former outlaw Evan Farris, answered the door. Muffled voices carried through the house as Budd threw back the covers.

He lumbered over to the bedchamber door and opened it before Sheriff Dawson could let himself in. "What is so important that you had to wake us at this ungodly hour, Sheriff?"

"There's been an attack on a stagecoach," Dawson answered. "The first one since you ran those bandits out of town. Mr. Thayer says he wants you to look into it with me."

"Do you think it's them?"

"Only one way to find out." The lawman shrugged.

Budd tucked in his shirt and grabbed a vest from the pile of clothes strewn about the room. He grimaced at his reflection as he caught sight of himself in the mirror.

Work had been hard, but being in Sacramento was even harder for him as of late. Each time he laid eyes on Rose Buchanan, it reminded him of all the times his mistakes had caught up to him. Knowing she was married to his old friend Douglas was like a knife to his heart.

Budd quickly fastened his vest and followed the sheriff out to the horses. He took his time and whispered softly into his mare's ear as he patted her on the side. She was as wild and stubborn as her rider, but fiercely loyal. "That's my girl. You're more than I deserve, Ivory."

"Can we get moving, Mr. Mansfield?"

"I don't know if I trust a man who ain't sweet to his mare," Budd chuckled in jest. He pulled himself onto Ivory's saddle.

"I got to ask, Sheriff. How are things going with Evan as your new deputy? He seems eager to prove himself."

Sheriff Dawson hesitated. He scratched at his stubbled chin and pointedly ignored Budd's prying gaze. "I, uh, I don't think he has what it takes to be a man of the law, Mr. Mansfield. He's… untamed, if you will.

The man has a tendency to call in favors from outlaws, and I just don't want my men associated with unsavory characters."

"It's his experience as an outlaw that made him an invaluable asset in my investigation into the stagecoach robberies," Budd reminded him. "Even an upstanding citizen like Mr. Thayer respects Evan's abilities."

"It isn't his skill that worries me, Mansfield. It's the fact he shows no regard for the rules." Sheriff Dawson gestured to the folks milling about the town as they rode through the heart of Sacramento. "These people trust I will keep them safe. It is both an honor and a burden I carry with me each day I put on this badge. And I can maintain that trust because I follow the rules of the law."

Not even Budd gave much thought to the system the leaders of this ever-expanding nation had put that in place. Evan Harris, on the other hand, was aware of the laws and still found creative ways to bend them to his will.

It was part of the reason Budd trusted his friend so much. He relied on Evan to do what was right to get the job done, but also to do what was necessary to save lives. Sheriff Dawson was a strict man—a fair man, but strict.

Budd reached over and slowed the sheriff's horse. He held nothing but sincerity in his eyes as he met the sheriff's gaze. "Evan could have run," he said. "He put his life at risk to help us, and he stuck around after the dust cleared, even though he could have been arrested. At least give him that."

"Commendable. However, he would not be a deputy in my town without you and Mr. Thayer speaking on his behalf." The sheriff gave Budd one of his famous no-nonsense looks that ended the conversation.

It wasn't difficult to understand where the lawman was coming from, but Evan was Budd's friend, and he had no choice but to defend him.

Despite what Sheriff Dawson or Budd's employer at Pratt Dempcy thought, Evan Farris was a good man who deserved their respect as much as their tolerance.

The sounds of construction drew Budd away from his thoughts and back to reality. A cloud of dirt hovered around the build site as men hammered away at large iron nails.

Rows of workers hauled planks of wood, strips of metal, and tools as the railway slowly grew longer and longer. A couple of yards away was a stagecoach turned onto its side. A stagecoach surrounded by bodies, either dead or injured.

"My god," Budd exclaimed. He eased Ivory off to the side and jumped from the saddle.

Sheriff Dawson was close behind. They approached the coach with caution, guns drawn and eyes sharp. Movement caused the curtain to ,flutter and Budd raised his gun.

"Come out slowly and raise your hands."

The door to the stagecoach pushed open. and pale, thin hands appeared. A woman with flaming red hair crawled out of the cabin. Her bottom lip trembled, but she raised her head proudly as her arms lifted.

"They came out of nowhere," the woman said. "We were just riding and then… t-they shot the driver. I saw evil in their eyes, mister."

He holstered his gun and gestured for the woman to come closer. Out of the corner of his eye, Budd spotted an ace of spades pinned to the stagecoach with a throwing knife.

His stomach dropped. Sheriff Dawson must have noticed the gang's signature, for he let out a foul curse that caused Budd to wince.

***

The Old Mill

Smoke hovered in the air. Ripley Eagleson sat with his feet propped up on a table littered with stacks of cash, fine jewelry, and little trinkets. He wrapped his lips around the end of his cigar and inhaled deeply. Five men stood around him with black masks that dangled around their necks. Each one unloaded a bag filled with loot.

"When I was a child, my father read me a story about knights and their loyalty to their king," Rip said. "I didn't want to be a knight or a king like most young boys. I wanted to be the dragon." Rip stood up and ran a hand down the front of his finely tailored vest. He circled the men and continued, "You are the knights in my story, boys. And among you five is a king—a heroic leader who can take this godforsaken region and turn it into his castle. I've seen the potential each one of you has. So which of you is going to rise to the challenge?"

Hector Vasquez, Leroy Murphy, Salazar Torez, Charles Wright, and Pete Jones sized each other up with wicked ambition glimmering in their eyes. Salazar stepped forward.

Rip's eyes widened with interest. He tugged the black scarf from around Salazar's neck and pulled a red one from his back pocket. "You were the one who freed Pete from that rope. It's only fitting you wear the crown."

"Thanks, boss," Sal replied with a thick accent. "It was an honor."

Rip smiled as he wrapped the scarf around Sal's neck and tightened it. Sal's face turned white, and he struggled.

Rip threw his weight onto the man, pinning him to the floor as he fought for air. "Do you know what makes that story so special to me?" he hissed into Sal's ear. "The king is brave, but he is wise enough to still fear the dragon.

"Do you fear me, Salazar?"

"Sí!"

When Rip released Sal, a ragged cough filled the air. Sal doubled over onto his stomach, wheezing and gasping. Rip chuckled as he stood up and adjusted his suit. He clapped his hands before gesturing to the table behind him.

"Do not forget why you are all here," Rip said. "I have promised security and good fortune for your families, and I have kept my word. Now it is time to prove your loyalty once again."

A door opened at the far end of the old steel mill. Rip's sister Beatrice and her young daughter Kaitlyn appeared. The sinister smile on Rip's face melted away as he beheld his niece. He walked over to them and lifted the small child into his arms. Kaitlyn nuzzled her nose into her uncle's neck and yawned sleepily.

"Put the rest of the loot in the wagons. What's on this table is yours to split equally. Do with it what you please, but keep lying low while in the city, or else I'll have to put you down."

One by one, the outlaws filled their pockets and wandered outside to where a caravan awaited their arrival. Rip carried little Kaitlyn out to a wagon near the front gate and handed her back to her mother.

They piled three other wagons high with crates and chests, containing just a portion of Ripley Eagleson's wealth. There was no one he trusted more than Beatrice with his money.

"Mount up!" he shouted.

An older man with salt and pepper hair led a powerful stallion to Rip.

"Thank you, Jorge. I hope Storm hasn't given you too much trouble."

"No problem, señor."

Rip tossed a small money clip to his servant and swung his leg over Storm. He settled into the saddle before he whistled sharply through his teeth. Storm trotted along the path just beyond the sturdy walls of the Old Mill.

The wagons rattled, wheels turning as they rolled over jagged earth.

Beatrice eyed Rip from the back of the wagon. Her gaze cut deeply to the heart of the cruel gang leader. "I can't believe you," she sighed.

"Not this again."

"Yes, this again!" Beatrice pulled the wagon cover aside and leaned forward as she whispered harshly at her brother. "These men do not deserve what you are doing. They are counting on you to provide for their families.

Each time they ride out of that filthy mill, they put their lives in danger. And for what? Money they will never get to spend?"

"These men are killers and thieves, Beatrice," Rip snapped, though he kept his voice low enough only she heard him. "Don't tell me what they deserve."

"You got my husband killed for this money. Johnny is dead because of you and you've roped me into your schemes with lies and—"

Rip reached into the wagon and grabbed his sister's arm. He kept a close eye on Kaitlyn, where she slept with her head resting on Beatrice's lap. "I didn't hear you complaining when I bought you that ranch or when you were out spending my money on new dresses.

Budd Mansfield knows you lied for Johnny, and he'll question you the second he gets the chance. You're leaving town, Beatrice, and that's the end."

She pressed her lips into a thin line and jerked her arm out of his grasp. "Fine," Beatrice huffed. "You trust me, so I'll trust you."

Rip nodded and closed the back of the wagon to shield his family from sight. He circled the front of the caravan, eyes peeled as he watched the horizon.

They riddled the area with those looking to attack unsuspecting travelers. Given the choice between Budd Mansfield and some bushwhackers, however, Rip would have chosen the latter.

There was just something about Budd Mansfield that made Rip uneasy. Perhaps it was the shifty eyes or mysterious past—either way, once Mansfield realized Rip's gang was robbing coaches again, there was bound to be trouble.

Chapter 2

Railroad Construction Site
Sacramento, California

"It's going to take years before they finish the railroad to Black Lake and Timber," Sheriff Dawson muttered. "People still rely on Pratt Dempcy for stagecoaches and wagons. How are they supposed to feel safe when gangs are robbing them blind?"

The lawman dragged one of the dead men off to the side and closed the poor soul's eyes.

Someone in the gang had killed the driver, the shotgun rider, and one guard. It was a horrific sight that Budd wanted washed from his memory.

"You think this'll stop when the railway finishes?" Budd snorted bitterly. "I've seen what happens in train robberies, Sheriff. It ain't no better than what happened here. Just more people to rob."

The smell of death caused Budd's gut to clench and roil. He kneeled beside the shotgun man and inspected the wounds. Short, straight lines peppered the man's torso.

"He was stabbed. They shot the other two," Budd announced. "Whoever killed him wanted him to die slowly. This... this ain't just a robbery gone bad."

"We had six stagecoaches reach Sacramento this week. Only Pratt Dempcy's coach was attacked," Sheriff Dawson replied. "Are you sure it's the same gang?"

Budd stood up and pointed to the playing card pinned to the frame of the stagecoach. "The ace of spades is an omen of death. It spreads fear, to tell someone that death is coming for them. The gang I've been after uses it as their signature—as a warning to Pratt Dempcy."

Sheriff Dawson nodded his head, along with Budd's explanation. "Why stab this man and not the others?"

"I'm not sure. But we need to get these men to the coroner. Their families will want a funeral." Budd stepped carefully as he made his way over to the woman and man who survived the attack. Both passengers sat on the side of the road with at least three feet of distance between them. However, Budd's keen eyes caught sight of matching wedding bands on their fingers.

"Pardon me," he said. "But I need to ask you a few questions."

"When can we leave?" shouted the man. "I am Bernard Wilson of Wilson's Coal Company, and I demand to be treated with the respect I am due." Mr. Wilson stumbled to his feet and jabbed his finger in the center of Budd's chest.

Budd swatted the man's hand aside. "Wait for the deputies to arrive with the wagon. We'll get you and Mrs. Wilson situated as soon as we are able."

"You expect me to ride with these dead men?"

The horrified look on Mr. Wilson's face triggered something in Budd. He snatched the scrawny little pest by the front of his tailored suit and slammed him on the ground. "These men died protecting you!"

Sheriff Dawson grabbed onto Budd and yanked him back, dislodging the grip he had on the man's coat. "Enough! Do nothing stupid."

Budd was like an enraged bull. "Wayne Ervin, Nile Holmes, and Jesse Thomas! They had names. They had families, Dawson, and they died for that piece of—"

"Stop, Mansfield." The sheriff held Budd back and kept him from throttling Mr. Wilson. "We got a job to do."

Though Budd was nearly a foot taller than Dawson, he backed down with little fight. He respected the lawman. If not for that respect, Budd would have knocked Mr. Wilson's teeth down his throat.

"I am the manager of security with Pratt Dempcy," he said. "I hired these men to guard stagecoaches. Their deaths... are on my hands, not yours, Mr. Wilson. Please accept my apologies."

"I will take it under consideration." Bernard Wilson dusted off his coat and sauntered over to his young wife. "They will award my forgiveness when you retrieve our belongings and the money that was stolen."

Budd shoved down the urge to throttle Mr. Wilson. Thankfully, the deputies arrived with the wagon. Evan rode ahead with a rifle perched in his lap. Budd noticed how his friend's eyes widened at the sight of the carnage laid out on the road.

A few of the deputies bowed their heads and said a silent prayer. Though the fallen men had been employed by Budd, they had also been part of Sacramento's community.

"Get the bodies to the coroner and the passengers to the inn," Sheriff Dawson ordered his men. "I'm sure Mansfield will want to question them."

Budd walked away from the small group of people and approached Mrs. Wilson.

"Ma'am, I'm sorry about my disagreement with your husband, but I have to ask you something real important." He reached into his satchel and pulled out a small, yellowed drawing of an eagle tattoo. "Did you see anything similar to this inked on the bandits?"

Mrs. Wilson shook her head. "They wore all black. Long sleeves, gloves, masks…"

"Think real hard, Mrs. Wilson. Is there anything that might help us figure out who these men are?"

The woman chewed her swollen bottom lip as she pondered. "The man with the knife… Pale hair and dark eyes," Mrs. Wilson said finally. "Almost black. He was like a demon. I swear he peered right into my soul."

No one came to mind at the description. Budd wrote down every detail, fully intending to question Bernard Wilson at a later date.

He tucked away the drawing of John Pepper's tattoo and rode back to town with the wagon.

Evan hadn't said a word since he saw the dead stagecoach guards. Budd understood. He was the sort of man who buried his guilt until it ate at him from the inside.

He wondered for a moment whether the leader of the bandits was capable of such empathy. Many of the victims of past robberies described the bandit leader as charismatic and fair—not at all what Budd expected.

Not at all the sort of man who condoned the violence displayed that day.

***

Pratt Dempcy & Company Office
Sacramento, California

The office was small and tidy, just like the man behind the desk. Budd smiled when Howard Thayer glanced up at him through his round spectacles. There was just something about the man that made Budd trust him.

Without Mr. Thayer, he would never have gotten a job with the stagecoach company.

"Mansfield, dear boy! How splendid it is to see you!"

"Hello, Mr. Thayer. I'm afraid this ain't a social call," Budd replied grimly. "There was an attack on one coach headed to town."

Mr. Thayer's smile fell instantly. "Oh, my heavens. Is everyone safe?"

"We lost three men. Both passengers are alive. They injured two of the guards but they're doing fine." Budd shuffled his feet and crossed his arms over his chest. "Bernard Wilson may file a complaint with the sheriff."

Though it paled compared to the first one, Mr. Thayer's smile returned as he replied, "I'm sure his strongly worded opinion was not a contributing factor to the incident at all. Worry not, my boy. It is in the past now."

Budd swallowed down the urge to chuckle and watched as his employer dug around in the desk for something. Seconds later, Mr. Thayer brought out a map of the California territory marked with several lines and symbols.

"What is this?"

"Duncan came to me with alternative travel routes last month," said Mr. Thayer. "Once you've hired new men, I'll need you to ensure each road is safe. Any sign of bandits and I want the route closed."

Budd whistled as he glanced down at the map. "There are only four routes left, sir. Can we afford to lose another?"

"After what happened last year, the company isn't taking any more risks. The lives of our passengers are top priority." Mr. Thayer pointed to a route marked in red ink.

"I want you to ride with the transport to Reno. The city is expanding, and officials have asked that we provide safe passage until they complete construction this winter."

"Can't they use the trains?"

"Some of their more esteemed citizens are refusing to ride with the railroad workers and the miners," Mr. Thayer grumbled. "We have arranged private coaches."

"That means a big payoff for any gang looking to rob us." Budd paced back and forth in front of the desk. "I'll go, but I need to make arrangements for my men who were killed."

"Nonsense. I will handle everything and make sure we rightly compensate the families for their losses." Mr. Thayer removed his spectacles. "Just do everything to ensure this does not happen again, Mr. Mansfield."

Budd accepted the map from Mr. Thayer with a quick nod and walked out the office. He stepped out into the sunlight, basking in the fresh air for the first time that morning.

Ivory nudged his arm with her snout, and he rewarded her with an oatcake from his satchel. He spoiled the mare beyond belief, but one look in her eyes eased the guilt that weighed on Budd's shoulders. Even if it was only a little.

He stopped a young boy on the sidewalk. "Want to make a few coins?"

The child looked thrilled by the prospect, jumping up and down with a bright smile on his cherub face. "Really, mister? I would! I would!"

Budd handed the lad a few dollars and said, "Put up notes at the post office, sheriff's office, and the general store to let folks know Pratt Dempcy & Company are looking for workers. Come see me at the eatery when you're finished, and I might have another dollar for you."

As the child scampered off, Budd made his way home to the small house he shared with his friend Evan Farris. It had been a week since Rose and Douglas moved to their new estate, and Budd missed her more and more each day.

Sometimes he caught himself dreaming of a different life, one where it had been him who married Rose and not Douglas, but it was a fool's dream. Budd never wanted their friendship to suffer on account of his feelings for her. A married lady of society had no need for someone like him.

Just as Budd suspected, Evan greeted him at the door before he had the chance to announce himself. The newly deputized man glared at Budd from beneath the brim of his hat as Budd tended to Ivory. He scraped out her horseshoes with his knife, removed the saddle, and led her to the drinking trough. "What is it, Farris?"

"You agreed to ride with the next transport."

"I did," Budd stated simply. "It's my job to do these things. Besides, I'm down three men as of this morning."

"Two."

Budd glanced at Evan from over his shoulder and smiled. "I suspected you might want to come along. What does the good sheriff have to say about that?"

"He understands it's something I need to do. We started this together, Budd. I ain't going to let you have all the fun," Evan snorted. "And I know some guys who might—"

"No."

"Hear me out."

"No hired guns," Budd said. "I want men who will understand what we're up against. Men who won't leave us high and dry if a better offer is made."

Evan grabbed Budd gently by the shoulder. "Stop being so darn stubborn and just listen! I know these people, all right? All I'm asking is that you give them the same chance you gave me."

Budd lowered Ivory's hooves back to the ground and tucked his knife away. "They got bounties?"

"Not in this territory."

Until he found time to train additional guards, Budd couldn't be picky. He reckoned Evan's trust was enough to go by. After all, their run-in with a mercenary named Sadey Conner hadn't gone horribly wrong although they had hired her to kill Budd. "Introduce us after you and I ride to Reno."

Chapter 3

The Trail to Reno, Nevada

Six masked bandits slowed their horses near the crossroads. One broke off from the group and rigged a stick of dynamite to a boulder. The others remained in their saddles, eyes glued to their leader as he rode down the path toward a stagecoach in the distance.

An explosion turned the boulder into rubble, sending chunks of rock flying. Smoke swirled around the bandits, shrouding them in darkness, as the stagecoach came to a stop.

Rip smiled behind his mask. He raised his revolver and fired three times. "Drop the key to the strongbox onto the ground," said Rip to the stagecoach driver. "I don't want anyone getting hurt, so do as I say."

Smoke cleared. Large rocks blocked the road, so the stagecoach had to retreat or go through the bandits.

Rip rode up beside the coach and holstered his weapon. He lowered his voice and added a slow, Southern drawl. "My men ain't goin' to wait much longer. Get the key or somebody is—"

The door opened, cutting off the threat that hovered on the bandit's lips. Budd Mansfield emerged from the shadows, larger than life. He unfolded his long limbs as he stepped out of the cabin. "This stagecoach is the property of Pratt Dempcy & Company, and it is under my protection."

"Do you surrender?"

"No." Mansfield pushed Rip right out of the saddle. "Do you surrender?"

Rip rolled to the right and jumped to his feet. Budd Mansfield's gun brushed Rip's cheek. A bang caused his ears to ring as the bullet just barely missed his face.

Rip raised his fists in a fighting posture and punched Mansfield in the jaw three times in rapid succession. The tall man buckled under the force of the hits, buying Rip time to retreat.

"Get the box open!" he shouted to his men. "And kill anyone who tries to stop you."

The masked bandits descended upon the stagecoach like a plague of locusts. They tore off the doors and pulled the passengers out of their seats.

Budd Mansfield climbed to his feet before he charged after Sal—who stood over a young woman with a knife.

With Mansfield distracted, Rip circled the stagecoach. He watched as Leroy broke open the strongbox and stuffed money into a burlap sack. "Hurry before reinforcements arrive!"

Hector and Charles held the driver at gunpoint. The passengers wept openly, slobbering all over themselves with fear.

Rip caught the loot bag Leroy tossed him and whistled for Storm. Budd Mansfield's shotgun man fired at Leroy, but the blast failed to hit its mark.

Storm huffed through his nostrils as Rip pulled himself into the saddle. He spun his horse around and opened his mouth to give orders. But words never left his lips as he spotted Pete less than a foot from Budd Mansfield. The outlaw hesitated, lowering his weapon slightly before he raised it again.

Rage coursed through Rip's veins like frigid water. "Ride out!"

Charles kicked the driver in the head, knocking the man unconscious. Hector wrangled Pete and Leroy back toward the horses as Rip kept his gun aimed at Budd Mansfield. They locked eyes over the mask.

Rip cocked his revolver and watched a look of pure defiance enter the other man's gaze. Still, there was no recognition. No sign Mansfield had identified him as the leader of the gang.

Rip remembered the first time they crossed paths. Budd Mansfield had walked into Haven Ranch as if he owned the land. There was a formidable presence about him that defied his usual serene expression.

But Rip had seen Mansfield in a fight. He knew what sort of monster dwelled beneath those calm waters. There was no doubt in Rip's mind that Mansfield could have taken most of his gang out if not for his need to protect the passengers.

The sound of hooves broke through Rip's thoughts, bringing his mind to the present. Hector led the way as they headed back to the Old Mill.

Rip covered the rear. His gun remained firmly in his grasp until they reached the outskirts of Yosemite Valley.

It was nearly nightfall by the time the walls of the old factory came into view.

Rip finally holstered his revolver. "Pete, hang back. The rest of you need to count the loot and the ammunition. Don't miss a single item."

An unsettling silence fell over the group. One by one, Rip's men disappeared into the Old Mill except for Pete.

The young outlaw shook nervously beside the horses. "D-did I do somethin' wrong, boss?" Pete stuttered. "I thought things went as well as expected."

Rip lowered himself from the saddle in one fluid motion. He removed his gloves one finger at a time while walking slowly toward Pete.

And though his ears still rang from Budd Mansfield's gun discharging near his face, Rip still heard the fleshy thud of his fist as it connected with Pete's cheek. The outlaw fell backward and tripped over a bucket of water.

Rip kicked him while he was on the ground.

"You could have shot him," he snarled. "You could have saved me the trouble of killing Mansfield, but you let him live!"

"I'm sorry!"

"Not yet, you ain't." Rip tangled his fingers in the front of Pete's shirt and pulled him up toward his face. When they were just inches apart, Rip continued, "He killed my brother-in-law, and he shut down my operation for months. Next time the opportunity to avenge Johnny's death presents itself, you take it."

"Yes, boss."

Rip released his hold on Pete and scowled down at the pathetic outlaw. "No one—and I mean no one—gets paid for this job. I wonder how Salazar will feel when I tell him he has you to thank for that."

***

Timber, California
Two days later

The doors to the saloon banged against the wall as Budd Mansfield entered. Heads turned in his direction. Budd paid them no mind.

He clenched his bruised jaw and swaggered over to the table where Evan Farris sat with two other men.

"Your contacts are Blake and Steven Wright?" Budd scoffed. "I expected mercenaries, but not famous mercenaries."

Evan's crooked grin made Budd roll his eyes. "The second transport made it to Reno yesterday. Seems the gang took the bait."

"They nearly killed those saloon girls," Budd replied. "I had to pay Katherine twice the amount we promised."

"But the job got done. The outlaws didn't attack the right stagecoach, so your plan worked." Evan snapped his fingers and ordered a round of beers for the table.

The Wright brothers sat in their chairs with grim expressions on their faces. It was a stark contrast to Evan's persistently jovial demeanor.

"So, Evan says you boys are worth hiring." Budd leaned over the table a bit as he spoke. "This is a complicated situation. We need to maintain a delicate balance with the law, or else Sheriff Dawson will call in a marshal."

Steven's expression softened a touch as he replied, "Actually, we were hopin' you could help us the way you helped Evan."

"What?"

"We want out," said Blake. "It's been nine months since our last contract, but we can't get work otherwise. Bounty huntin' ain't so different from gunslingin'… We ain't even goin' to try that. Too much temptation."

"You want to be deputies?" Budd questioned.

Both brothers shook their heads, but it was Blake who answered. "We want to work with you. In that delicate balance you mentioned."

Budd wrapped his fingers around his beer and took a swig as he thought to himself. There was a lot at stake. Pratt Dempcy trusted him with the safety of their passengers, as well as the varying wealth they traveled with.

The Wright brothers were known for their cunning ways, their ability to manipulate anyone. "First, let's talk about the gang," Budd suggested. "Any thoughts on them?"

"We heard about a stagecoach robbery that went down last year. They attacked the coach on the way to Timber. Things got messy," Steven said as he lowered his voice. The deep tone vibrated in the space between them.

"They fled from the scene, and they captured two of their men at the border."

"I was on that stagecoach. It was the day I got hired by Pratt Dempcy. They were ruthless. But somewhere along the lines, they changed. People started respecting the men who robbed them of their valuables. It was unsettling at first, but it seems they're back to their old ways again. You got names?"

"Rumors say it was Salazar Torez and our older brother, Charles, who were arrested at the border," Blake explained.

"We can't be sure, but there was talk that the two of them escaped the jailhouse a few weeks ago and were last seen in a small town called Black Lake. It's not too far from here. About two miles, give or take."

"Going after family ain't ever easy." Budd took another sip of his beer to settle the knot in his belly. "You two sure you want to—"

"Never been more sure in our lives," Blake interjected. "It's because of Charles, why we're wanted in three territories. He uses our names.

All we want is a chance to start over, to clean up our reputations and do somethin' honorable for a change."

Evan, who had been uncharacteristically quiet through the entire conversation, piped in at last. "I see this as a situation where everyone gets what they want," he said as he gestured excitedly. "They get to prove themselves to the well-meaning members of society. I get to earn the favor of our dear sheriff, and you get enough men to guard the stagecoaches.

It ain't perfect, but it sure as hell ain't bad, either."

"All right," Budd began. "We'll work together under one condition."

Evan, Blake, and Steven turned their attention to Budd and Budd alone. It was as if the world around them had shrunk back into nothingness.

They had not even noticed the fresh beers passed around the table by a soiled dove who worked in the saloon.

Budd Mansfield wet his dry mouth with a quick drink before he continued. "No one else dies. Not us, not the passengers, and not the bandits," he asserted. "We save everyone so that the gang doesn't go out the easy way. They make it to trial, no matter what."

Each of them nodded their heads in agreement.

The only one who hesitated was Steven. "We might not have told you everythin' we heard about the gang."

"Then speak up now before I change my mind."

Steven scratched his beard and leaned back in his seat. "They have a coach. One of Pratt Dempcy's."

Budd didn't like the sound of that. He scooted his beer away to clear his mind and met Steven's gaze from across the table. "What about it?"

"There were a few hired guns in here a while back talkin' about bandits movin' guns in a Pratt Dempcy coach," Steven informed Budd. "If it's the same bandits you're after..."

"Then they might be preparing to hit the company in a big way," Budd added. He had seen what the gang was capable of with only six men and a few pistols.

An entire shipment of guns was enough firepower to take on the entire city of Sacramento. "These men who have returned. Salazar Torez and Charles Wright. What can you tell me about them?"

"Charles is a coward, but a dang good thief," Steven said. "He can steal just about anythin'. Heck, he'd take the watch off a preacher's wrist and sell it back to him without the poor man bein' aware he was gettin' worked."

Blake looked uneasy. His leg bounced anxiously beneath the table, causing the bottles to rattle. "It's Sal you gotta worry about."

"Why him specifically?"

"He's a cold-blooded killer," Blake answered. "Uses a knife so he can look his prey in the eyes as they die."

"One of our men was stabbed to death during a stagecoach robbery a few days ago."

Blake looked Budd straight in the eyes and said, "Then you need us to help you—to make sure no one else suffers like that again."

Chapter 4

It was a quiet morning when Budd arrived in Sacramento. He reckoned it might be his last time in the city for a while, so he took a moment and enjoyed the peaceful hour.

A bit of dew covered the shop windows as the fog thinned. He breathed in air that smelled of chimney smoke and rain. Even Ivory seemed calmer than usual.

"Mansfield," called Sheriff Dawson from the front porch of the sheriff's office.

Budd slowed his horse and hitched the reins to the post nearby. "Got any news?"

"Deputy Farris and I have been asking around," said the lawman. "No one wanted to come forward at first. Last night I got a visit here at the office from Miss Georgia James. She's the schoolteacher."

"What's she got to do with stagecoach robberies?" Budd followed the sheriff inside and scraped the mud off his boots. He plopped down into the chair in front of Dawson's desk.

The office was quiet. There were no prisoners in the cells or deputies around.

"They held Miss James at gunpoint during one attack. Says she might help," replied Sheriff Dawson. "Figured you could question her yourself, so she's on her way here."

Just then, the bell above the door chimed. Budd turned his head toward the sound and spotted a petite woman at the entrance.

She fidgeted with her bonnet before offering her hand. "You must be Mr. Mansfield."

Budd stood up and returned the polite gesture. "I suppose I must be. The sheriff said you might have some information for me."

He motioned toward the chair he had vacated, and Miss James took his place.

"Oh, I sure do hope I can help."

He skipped the rest of the pleasantries and got right to the point. "Can you identify any of the men?"

"Yes, I believe I can. He looked... well, he looked like Leroy Murphy," Miss James insisted. "He comes by the schoolhouse and pesters me. I recognized the scar above his brow. It was dark when it happened, but I'm sure it was him."

Budd listened closely as Miss James continued her description of Leroy Murphy and the likeness he shared with the bandit. Sheriff Dawson, of course, wasn't thrilled by the idea of the Murphy family being tied up in the stagecoach robberies.

It seemed as if every member of that ill-bred family was up to no good in Sacramento. Every week, Sheriff Dawson dragged another Murphy into a cell but murder wasn't usually on their list of crimes.

The C-shaped scar was the only lead. Sure, Blake and Steven had told him they suspected their brother was involved, but Budd needed more to go on than a hunch.

There were days when he followed his gut and times when he let the facts speak for themselves.

He couldn't afford to take any more chances. "Thank you, Miss James."

Georgia James saw herself out. She waved goodbye to Budd and the sheriff, leaving them to process the information she offered.

Sheriff Dawson stood up from his desk and pinned a note to the board beside the door. "I'll get someone to draw up a picture matching the description and put it on a wanted poster."

"Before I go," Budd said. "Had there been any reports of a stolen coach from Pratt Dempcy back before I got hired?"

The sheriff walked over to his cabinet of files. He flipped through a couple before he found a wrinkled sheet of paper. "One. A mercantile coach was stolen."

Budd cursed under his breath. He knew from experience that Pratt Dempcy had some of the largest transport coaches available to merchants.

Though they were smaller than most wagons, there was plenty of room for whatever the gang might have had planned. "Thank you, Sheriff. I'm grateful for your help."

"Just buy me a drink when these criminals are brought to justice," retorted Sheriff Dawson.

Budd took his leave, making his way toward the Murphy farm on the outermost part of town. It was a modest farm with a few cows and some crops.

From the outside, it looked normal, nice even, but Budd knew what went on within the walls of the old farmhouse. The lot of them were a bunch of snakes, scheming and stealing from anyone who had the misfortune of meeting them.

Each one was a low-life criminal that made Budd feel sorry for the lawmen of Sacramento.

Still, he had a job that needed doing, so he followed the lead provided by Georgia James all the way out to the Murphy Farm. The smell of cow dung burned Budd's eyes as he approached the front porch.

An older woman sat in a rocking chair with a cigarette between her lips. "That's far enough," she said. "What brings you here?"

Budd lowered his foot from the first step. "Ma'am, my name is—"

"I know what your name is. I asked what brings you here."

"Well, I represent Pratt Dempcy, and we're currently investigating a string of stagecoach robberies," Budd replied irritably. He pulled his hat low to hide the scowl on his face. "Is Leroy Murphy home, ma'am?"

"My son's whereabouts ain't no concern of yours."

The upstairs curtain opened slightly, and Budd caught sight of Red Murphy. He beckoned the youngest of the Murphy brothers down.

Red looked a bit disgruntled, but he eventually met Budd at the front steps. "What do you want?" Red hissed. "Last time I saw you, I got locked away for kidnappin' that maid."

"Wish I could say I was sorry, but that'd be a lie. You got off easier than you deserved." Budd took a step closer to Red. He glared up at him, silently daring the man to make a false move.

"Why are you here, Mansfield?"

Budd grabbed Red by the shirt. "I'm here for your cousin. Where's Leroy?"

***

Bull Trotter Saloon
Timber, California

Scantily clothed saloon girls draped themselves across Ripley Eagleson as he sipped his bourbon. Thin, pale fingers curled around his necktie. Sensual giggles and lush curves surrounded him.

The only problem was that Rip's mind wasn't on the ladies or the drink in his hand. No, he riveted his attention to the man who had just sauntered into the upstairs parlor of the saloon. Salazar had left the bar with a woman and returned alone.

"Let me remind you we are lying low," Rip said.

Salazar grabbed a bottle from the tray of drinks beside the rest of the gang and took a seat on a red settee. "Now, what's that supposed to mean? I put Caroline to bed, just like you told me to. They *are* under our protection, ain't they?"

Rip dismissed the women from the room with a single look. He ran his fingers through his raven-black locks that were slicked back from his face and held in place by pomade. The ointment smelled earthy.

It stuck to his fingers as he stood up from his seat and adjusted his vest. The garment was black with thin blue stripes, and it was worth more money than his men had made in an entire month. Rip's handcrafted cufflinks and watch were gold plated while the gang wore clothing from the local shops.

He was a man above the rest, after all.

"If Caroline doesn't return to her duties here in the saloon tomorrow night, then I'll go looking for her," Rip said to Salazar. "And if I find her dead, then you won't—"

"She is not dead."

"Then why is she not here?" he questioned.

Salazar's laughter boomed through the room, cutting off the nearby conversations. "I'm thinking you don't trust me. My feelings might get hurt, boss."

"What did you do to Caroline?"

"She slapped me, so I carved her face up a bit," Salazar chuckled.

Rip spun his revolver out of the holster and pressed the muzzle of the gun against Salazar's forehead. "These girls give us information because we keep them safe." He cocked the hammer back. "I'm a man of my word, Sal. If you make this town think I don't keep my promises, then I'll deliver your head to the sheriff in good faith."

"Take it easy, boss... No need to do anything crazy."

He kept the gun firmly in place as he replied, "I did not accept this sort of behavior from Johnny when he was alive, so I won't accept it from you.

If Mansfield hadn't killed that madman, I would have eventually done it myself. Do we understand each other?"

"Sí."

Rip moved the gun off to the side, less than an inch from Salazar's ear, and squeezed the trigger.

Screams from downstairs reached the parlor, but Rip didn't care. He looked on as Sal curled up in a ball on the floor with a smile on his face.

The other members of the gang glanced away from Sal and Rip, busying themselves with cards or dominos. Rip figured they must have finally found some common sense.

He grabbed his coat and holstered his gun. "Leroy, you and I need to have a conversation. Walk with me to the inn," Rip ordered. "Now."

Leroy hurried to grab his money from the card table before he followed Rip out the back door. They walked down the stairs in silence, but when their feet touched the ground, it was all business.

"What's goin' on, sir?" Leroy asked.

"My contacts in Sacramento said the passengers we were after made it to Reno. We robbed the wrong stagecoach."

"You sure? W-we got a lot of money out of that strongbox..."

Rip nodded his head. "I'm sure," he said confidently. "Which means Pratt Dempcy no longer cares about the money."

"Why wouldn't they care?"

"I don't know," Rip answered. "But I intend to find out. Have one of the girls in Sacramento send Budd Mansfield a letter from me. Tell him I want to meet."

"I don't know if that's a good idea, boss. He might set a trap." Leroy hurried to keep up with Rip's long stride. He was panting and out of breath by the time they reached the inn. "Or he'll just take the girl."

"Unlike you, he's a man of honor. Mansfield will know that lives are on the line, and if he makes one false move, we'll slaughter the whole town."

Rip pushed open the door to the inn and tipped his hat to the man behind the desk. He continued to his room and unlocked the door.

Leroy waited impatiently inside as Rip wrote a letter to Budd Mansfield. "I don't know about this, Rip. We might bring the law down on us."

"Dawson wouldn't dare risk any more deputies. Mansfield is on his own if he meets with us, and that's exactly how I want this to happen."

Rip used a golden press with a spade symbol to stamp the envelope closed with wax. "Deliver this to Darla at the Iron Stallion. Have her give it directly to Budd Mansfield and no one else."

Leroy took the envelope and hurried out of Rip's room. Once alone, Rip stripped away the layers of his facade. Gone were the golden cufflinks and watch, gone were the fine leather shoes, and gone were the confident smile and bright eyes of a gang leader.

Instead, Ripley Eagleson wore a stony expression. He was the cold, ruthless man only his sister had ever truly seen.

If not for his carefully crafted image, Rip knew the world would have feared him. He was the sort of man who could take over dynasties and bend others to his will with a single snap of his fingers.

Budd Mansfield had made himself an enemy. Rip was merely a predator responding to a threat in his territory.

Chapter 5

The door opened to reveal a grandiose entrance hall that made Budd's home feel like a hovel by comparison. He stepped over the threshold with his heart on his sleeve and his tongue firmly between his teeth, for he knew he could never trust himself around Rose.

She turned him into a blubbering fool whenever they were near one another. No other woman had ever made Budd feel so… conflicted. Part of him knew her marriage to his friend Douglas was nothing more than an arrangement—a contract between two desperate people.

Still, it was Rose's face Budd saw when he closed his eyes at night.

There were days when he wished he was young again. They had been closer back when they hadn't had to worry about grown-up things—when the world was simpler and a reputation he couldn't avoid hadn't tainted him in her eyes.

His employment with the Pinkertons hadn't gone over too well with Rose. She saw him as only a dog trained to do their dirty work. And she had been right to think such things.

But as he stood in her home, Budd felt like a stranger. He felt as if they hadn't been raised in the same orphanage or been friends at all.

She was a lady—married and beloved by all who knew her.

Budd was… well, at the end of the day he supposed not much had changed for him. The work he did for Pratt Dempcy came with a fancier title, but it was what it was: hunting men.

Perhaps if circumstances were different, if there wasn't a gang that tormented the stagecoach company, Budd could have been a normal man. A man good enough for Rose's love or friendship.

"Mansfield!" the joyous sound of Douglas's voice echoed in the entrance hall, thoroughly snapping Budd out of his daydreams. "Good to see you, old friend. It surprised me when you accepted our invitation to dinner."

"Things seem to have quieted down with work for the time being," Budd lied. The truth hadn't been so simple. In fact, he was certain Douglas wouldn't have taken kindly to being told Budd hadn't been able to spend one more second without seeing Rose.

And when she walked down the staircase in a powder-blue dress, he darn near stopped breathing. The light of the chandelier sparkled in her eyes, bringing back memories of summer days in the grain fields near the orphanage.

"Mr. Mansfield," Rose said quietly with a kind smile. She bowed her head politely.

Budd swallowed thickly. His tongue suddenly felt too large to speak. "Good to see you again, Mrs. Buchanan," he muttered after a few heartbeats. "You have a lovely home."

A servant led them into the dining room, where Budd was instructed to sit beside Douglas. He did as he was told, thankful for something to do other than gawk at Rose.

The cook seemed to have prepared a small feast for the three of them. Lamb, potatoes, greens, corn, bread rolls, and a hearty stew were served on silver platters. Budd felt like a fool in his denim pants.

Douglas filled the awkward silence with stories from his travels. The more he talked, the more Budd's attention strayed down dangerous paths. *Had Rose given him a lingering look?* he wondered to himself. *Had her foot grazed him beneath the table?*

"I heard you are searching for a gang of bandits, Mansfield," Douglas said suddenly.

Budd's head whipped toward his old friend, and he cleared his throat before he spoke. "I... yes, I am. Things are complicated, but I'm confident we are getting close."

"What is it you do for Pratt Dempcy again?" Rose asked, suddenly interested in the turn of conversation.

"I am the manager of security," Budd answered. "It's my job to make sure the stagecoaches arrive at their destinations safely and all of our passengers' belongings are accounted for. But right now, our primary concern is dealing with these bandits."

Douglas leaned back in his chair a bit and dabbed at the corner of his mouth with a napkin. "Dear lord! That sounds dangerous.

Can they not get the law to handle these ruffians? It hardly seems like it is your responsibility."

"I work with the full support of the lawmen in the area."

There was a scoff from Rose's side of the table that was hardly lady-like.

Budd bit the inside of his cheek and swallowed down his anger. "Sheriff Dawson is a friend of mine, and he works closely with Pratt Dempcy on this," he explained. "My partner, Evan Farris, was recently deputized."

"And you decided being a lawman was beneath you?" Rose's glib tone rubbed Budd the wrong way. She held her head high with an air of superiority that irked him.

"No, I decided the work I do is just as important, and the limitations of the law may not allow me to protect our clients," he said between tightly clenched teeth.

Budd stood up from the table and grabbed his jacket by the door. "I'll see myself out. I wouldn't want to overstay my welcome.

"It's clear this was more of a formality than a sincere invitation, anyway. Have a good night, Mr. and Mrs. Buchanan."

He slammed the door behind him on his way out and nearly leaped down the front steps. Budd wasn't sure what had come over him, but he felt as though a knife had been plunged into his heart.

Rose should have known him better than that. Shouldn't she? He knew it had been over a decade since they last saw each other, but she had written him letters over the years. Letters that were filled with kind words that made him believe there might have been at least a bit of residual fondness between them.

"I have a message for you, Mr. Mansfield," said a sultry voice as he turned the corner. Standing beneath a streetlamp was a beautiful blond woman with light freckles upon her nose. "The Blood Eagles request your presence."

***

Yosemite Valley, California

The sound of the waterfall reverberated off the nearby rocks. Budd stood beside the roaring rapids, cloaked in shadow beneath the moonless sky.

He thought back to the day he nearly died at the hands of the ruthless gang. Some nights, he awakened in a cold sweat, bellowing at the top of his lungs in fear of being pulled under the water once more.

The explosion had sent him over the waterfall at a terrifying speed.

And Budd never wanted to feel that afraid again. He remembered how it had felt when the waves crashed over his head and water filled his lungs. He remembered how his arms and legs had flailed wildly, trying to grab onto anything that might have slowed him down.

So when the gang leader chose that very spot for their meeting, Budd was more than a little hesitant. He had sent the woman named Darla back to her master with his response.

Budd had agreed to ride out to Yosemite Valley alone and under the shadow of night, with nothing to go on but a letter from a man claiming to be the leader of the gang he was after. It was a gamble.

It could have been a trap, for all he knew. But it was also a chance for him to see his enemy and look them in the eyes.

The eagle tattoo made more sense after Budd knew the name of the gang. He had heard of the Blood Eagles before, back when he had worked with the Pinkertons. It was a gang of ghosts.

Outlaws without known faces. They were famous, and yet no one had ever gotten close to identifying them or their leader. No one except Budd.

He checked his watch and grimaced. Nearly half past midnight, and the gang hadn't shown up. Budd was wondering if he had been the butt-end of a grim joke when he heard a whistle.

The forest went quiet.

Budd lowered his hand to his gun belt and listened to the faint sounds beyond the rushing water. He crept toward the tree line. Each step brought him closer to the unknown. "Who goes there?"

No one answered.

A loud crack echoed in his ears, and a sharp pain spread across the back of his skull. Budd collapsed, but he never hit the ground.

Large arms held him upright as they shoved a burlap sack down over his face. Someone hoisted him up onto a horse. Nausea churned in his belly.

Everything happened so fast. Budd hadn't had time to defend himself or speak. He blinked rapidly, but in the end, he succumbed to the darkness.

***

Budd Mansfield sat before him, tied to a rickety old chair. Rip snapped his fingers, and Leroy splashed Mansfield with a bucket of cold water. A dark stain spread along the floor of the abandoned cabin.

Rotted wooden planks squeaked in protest as Rip moved to stand over his prey. There was nothing to stop him from slitting Mansfield's throat. Nothing except his own pride, for he had given his word that Mansfield would leave there alive.

"Wake up," Rip said with an exaggerated drawl. It was as much a part of his disguise as the mask and gloves he wore. "Time for us to get down to business.

I've waited a long time for this."

Budd Mansfield stared around the cabin. Recognition sparked in his vivid blue gaze. "Is this about John Pepper?"

Those eerie eyes roamed over to the place where Johnny's body had been recovered, the place where Budd Mansfield had killed him.

"Nah," Rip snorted. "This is about the stagecoaches."

Mansfield fell silent.

Rip circled the man, taking in the sheer size of his opponent. "I'm going to give you an opportunity to stop the killings. No one else has to die. All you have to do is one little thing for me."

"And what would that be?" Mansfield asked.

"Stay out of my way." Rip stopped his circling. He pulled his revolver from the holster and handed it to one of his men.

"We will disarm ourselves and only take what's in the strongbox. All you have to do is look the other way, and your passengers will arrive safely."

"What about my workers? They have shot some of my guards and drivers dead because of your greed."

"They will live too," Rip replied. "So long as you do as I've asked. It's only money.

Surely you don't think it's worth the lives of your people. The insurance will reimburse them for whatever is lost."

Once again, only silence followed his words.

"I don't think you're understanding me," Rip snapped. "I'm givin' you a chance to save lives. Ain't that what they hired you for?" He picked up a plank of wood that leaned against the wall. He swung and bashed it over Mansfield's leg.

The men laughed as a broken shout filled the air. When Mansfield remained quiet, Rip hit him again.

The wood broke over his abdomen. Mansfield slumped over in the chair. He coughed raggedly and gasped for air. "All right! You got a deal," the man said finally. "I'll ignore the robberies, if you give me your word you'll stop the killings."

Rip smiled behind his mask. He gestured to his men, and they yanked Mansfield out of the chair. There was a bout of cruel laughter that welled inside of Rip, but he stamped it down.

There were few things in life he enjoyed more than making his enemy submit. "Mr. Mansfield, you will soon learn I am nothing if not a man of my word."

Chapter 6

Black Lake, California
June 1880

Dorothy "Dotty" Valentine stood beneath the shade of her royal blue parasol. She smiled at those who passed her by as she strolled along the sidewalk toward the stagecoach. A gentleman helped her into the coach with a proffered hand and a tip of his hat.

Dotty closed the parasol and laid it across her lap as the stagecoach lurched forward.

"Traveling alone?" asked the gentleman who sat opposite her. "I'm Louis. Louis Warren."

"I am, yes." Dotty turned her gaze to the town beyond the window, fully aware she had not offered her name. After all, it was better that few people know she traveled west. California differed from what the papers printed in the cities, for she saw no rivers of gold.

Instead, Dotty's amber gaze roamed over the dry, brittle earth as ripples of heat floated up from the many cracks.

She watched quietly as the town faded into a vast desert. Nothing but dirt and cacti between Black Lake and the mountains on the horizon.

But it wasn't what Dotty saw that worried her—no, it was what she heard that sparked fear in her heart. Three gunshots rang out.

Dotty lifted her skirt a bit and pulled her revolver from the holster strapped to her leg. Mr. Warren let out a startled cry and dropped to the floor of the stagecoach, cowering like a fool. The Valentines weren't the cowering sort.

"Get ready!" Dotty said as she pounded on the roof to alert the guards. "It's the Blood Eagles!"

The stagecoach sped up. Dotty leaned out the window and spotted three masked bandits riding hard after the stagecoach. Two more hung back with their rifles aimed at the guards on the roof.

The sixth rider stayed a few paces behind the others. She cocked her pistol and fired at the closest bandit. The bullet struck him in the shoulder, but it hardly slowed the bandit down.

"Get the girl!" the man shouted.

The rider at the rear spurred his horse on. He turned his enormous stallion and cut off the wounded bandit's path. They stopped, but the others continued after the stagecoach.

One bandit jumped onto the back of the stagecoach while the other two rode alongside it. Dotty pushed open the door, and it slammed into the side of one horse.

It bucked the rider out of the saddle.

Only three left.

"Hurry, Leroy!" shouted one bandit.

A victorious chuckle followed a loud pop. Dotty knew they had gotten the strongbox open.

The bandit named Leroy pulled stacks of money and golden nuggets out of the strongbox and stuffed them into a tan sack. Dotty climbed out onto the side of the stagecoach and took aim at the thief.

She squeezed the trigger, but the bullet missed. The bandit on the large stallion had knocked the gun from her hand. She hadn't seen him catch up with the others.

Dotty bit her lip to keep from cursing. She was better than some clumsy damsel, and her mistake might have cost her life. A gun. Dotty needed a gun, but the fierce wind nearly blew her down.

Her skirt flapped all around her legs as the driver fought to keep the coach moving. Dotty had only a split second before she tumbled to the ground.

She held her breath and climbed up onto the top of the stagecoach. To her surprise, the guards had not fired a single bullet at the bandits.

Dotty snatched a rifle from one man and turned to shoot the bandit named Leroy, but he was gone. Somehow, amid all the chaos, he had vanished.

She looked up and saw the six riders had gotten away. They rode off into the distance with everything—not that any of it belonged to her. Dotty had traveled to California with nothing but a gun, a parasol, and a second dress that was neatly tucked away in a small bag.

There was something awfully strange about the robbery.

"Why didn't you shoot?" she snapped angrily. "They were right there! You could have stopped this."

The guards shared a look she couldn't quite read. It was the driver who answered her question. "We have orders not to engage," he called as the stagecoach slowed to a crawl.

"The gang has killed our men before, and the boss thinks fighting escalated things. He wants us to keep driving… even if it means they get the money."

That… almost made sense in Dotty's mind. "How long until we get to Sacramento?" she asked.

"We're already there."

Dotty looked around at the city she had dreamed about. If not for her father's face on wanted posters, she would have traveled to Sacramento ages ago.

However, the Royal Heart Gang avoided California for the past five years because of a disagreement between her father and the Blood Eagles. So Dotty had traveled alone hoping to meet the man who had nearly brought the gang to their knees.

But after riding in a Pratt Dempcy stagecoach, Dotty wondered if perhaps her father's admiration of the famous Budd Mansfield was misplaced.

The coach pulled into the stables. Four workers hurried over to assist her. Dotty rolled her eyes and lowered herself down from the roof.

She opened the stagecoach and retrieved her bag and parasol. "Where can I find Budd Mansfield?"

"The boss is riding back from Timber. He should arrive soon. You can wait for him at the sheriff's office."

Dotty thanked the driver before she headed down the main road that cut through the city. Folks of all walks of life milled about without a care in the world. Dotty envied them.

She yearned for an ordinary life. Alas, her fate had been sealed the day she was born into the life of an outlaw.

For the first time in her life, she was happy when she saw the sheriff's office. Thankfully, it hadn't been too far from the stables.

Dotty opened the door and was assaulted by a cloud of cigar smoke. She waved a hand in front of her face before she approached the man behind the desk. He glanced up at her with a warm smile. "How can I help you?"

"Budd Mansfield owes me a new gun."

***

Sacramento, California

Thunder rumbled through the valley as lightning streaked across the sky. The smell of rain grew stronger, but Budd knew better than to get his hopes up. He clicked his tongue and eased Ivory into the stables. She tossed her mane, eager to get some much-deserved rest after the long ride from Timber. Budd had made up another excuse for why he hadn't ridden with yet another stagecoach.

That was four robberies in a single month.

Budd wasn't sure what the Blood Eagles had planned, but they had made a fool out of him. Even Mr. Thayer seemed to have lost faith in his ability to do his job over the weeks. It was a sharp blow to his pride, but it was a small price to pay for the lives that were spared. The hardest part was that he had lied to Evan more times than he could count.

So Budd simply swallowed his pride and kept his head down as he walked over to the sheriff's office. He avoided the sidelong glances from his men and the deputies. Only Steven and Blake Wright seemed to understand why he ordered the guards not to engage. Everyone else thought him a coward, assuming he had given up his fight against the gang. Only Budd knew the truth, and that was how he wanted it.

"Sheriff Dawson, I need to speak with you for a moment," he said as he entered the sheriff's office. Budd stopped just inside the doorway when a woman stood up from one chair. "Perhaps I'll come back another time. When you don't have a guest, I mean."

"Actually, Miss Dorothy Valentine is here for you," Sheriff Dawson explained. "She's the daughter of Theodore Valentine of the Royal Heart Gang."

"And what does that have to do with me, exactly?" Budd turned his gaze to the woman with dark hair and hazel eyes.

He recognized her father's name, but he never knew Theodore Valentine had a daughter. There was a slight resemblance that even he couldn't deny, but Budd thought she looked familiar to him somehow.

He tried to recall if they had met one desperate night or if they had crossed paths in Reno. Nothing came to mind.

"My father sent me here to help you," the woman said. "The Blood Eagles have been moving in on our territory for a long time, and he wants to help you bring them to justice... if you are willing to keep the Pinkertons off our trail, that is."

Budd shook his head. "I helped Evan Farris because he's a friend, and I'm helping the Wright boys because I need their help to guard the stagecoaches.

I'm not in the business of pardoning outlaws, Miss Valentine. I can't help your father."

"It isn't for him, Mr. Mansfield. It's for me. My father wants what's best for me, and I can't have a future if our family name is on every wanted poster from here to Texas," she replied.

"He's paid off the government, but the Pinkertons won't see reason."

"Well, I'm sorry, ma'am. I really am. But he should have been thinking about your best interest when he started robbing trains." Budd closed the door behind him and leaned over the sheriff's desk.

"If the Blood Eagles and the Royal Hearts are at war, I say we let them tear each other apart. I'll be happy to clean up the mess when it's over."

Sheriff Dawson crossed his arms over his chest and sighed. "That won't do. The law says we must capture and hold these men in our protection until they can go to trial. Now, I know you don't like—"

"To hell with what the law says!" Budd shouted. "The men who wrote those laws ain't out here fighting to save this land. They sit in their offices wearing fancy suits and talking about how to get richer. They ain't looking out for people like you and me, Dawson."

The sheriff stood up quickly. Papers flew off the desk as the chair scraped across the floor. Dawson's nostrils flared with unbridled rage. "We have been over this!"

"Gentlemen," Miss Valentine said. "I think I know how to settle this little dispute."

"And how is that?" Budd clenched his jaw so tight he feared his teeth might crack. He hooked his thumbs in his belt loops and stared down at the woman like she alone was the bane of his existence.

"They're always one step ahead."

"I know which road they will attack next."

Sheriff Dawson's and Budd's jaws dropped.

Miss Valentine opened the bag at her feet and revealed a small handwritten letter. "I have a friend in Timber who stole this off one of the Blood Eagles.

These are instructions to rob a stagecoach tomorrow morning on the road to Black Lake."

Budd inspected the letter. The same man who sent Budd the note about meeting at the waterfall had written it. "This... this might be our chance," he breathed in awe.

"If we take Calligan Road out past Oakhill Farm, there's a path that ain't on the region map. The stagecoach has a straight shot to Black Lake."

"You're willing to trust this woman?" Sheriff Dawson questioned.

"We need to try. If it doesn't work, then I may not get another shot at this. Once we know the road is safe, we can keep using it to transport the rest of our coaches."

Budd felt a spark of hope. He rushed over to the map behind the sheriff's desk and traced the aforementioned path with his finger. "It adds two miles to the ride, but it just might work."

Chapter 7

Budd Mansfield was not what Dotty ever expected. He seemed… human. The way outlaws talked about the tall, muscular man had made him a legend in the darker corners of the West.

He carried himself in a way that made Dotty think he wanted others to see him as an immovable obstacle. But she saw shadows in his eyes and scars upon his handsome face that proved he was indeed a mortal man.

"Where are you staying while you're in Sacramento?" Sheriff Dawson asked.

"My father arranged for me to stay with an associate of his. Mr. Douglas Buchanan purchased the Miller estate."

Dotty saw Mr. Mansfield flinch out of the corner of her eye. "His wife is graciously allowing me to work for a bed and meals."

"Are Rose and Douglas aware your father is a notorious gang leader?"

Dotty didn't answer Mr. Mansfield's question, for she didn't know for certain. After all, those who were ignorant to her father's work often assumed he was dead.

Though Dotty wasn't sure whether Budd Mansfield and her father's associate were well acquainted, it was obvious there was a bit of history between them. *Did he mention Mr. Buchanan's wife by name?* Dotty wondered.

His behavior was quite curious.

"Ignore Budd Mansfield when he's in these moods," the sheriff said. "He has a tendency to forget his manners when his focus is on protecting our citizens. I'm sure he would like to apologize for his behavior as he walks you to the Buchanans' home."

Budd Mansfield and Dotty locked eyes. Mr. Mansfield opened his mouth to protest, but the sheriff's tone left no room for argument.

Dotty clasped her bag shut and followed her reluctant escort outside. Rain began to fall the second she stepped over the threshold. Mr. Mansfield yanked her bag from her hand as she struggled to open her parasol.

He was the first man who didn't treat her like a doll made of porcelain. In some ways, she was grateful for his disinterest.

Dotty's shoes clicked on the sidewalk. The sound was nearly drowned out by the pitter-patter of the rainfall against rooftops. She found it all very soothing.

There was something rather peaceful about Sacramento—something that made it feel safer than Reno or the other cities she had lived in. Part of Dotty wondered if her newfound feeling of safety had to do with Mr. Mansfield's presence.

"Are you always so brooding?" she chuckled.

He scowled at her from over his shoulder.

"Oh, come now, Mr. Mansfield," Dotty said. "I'm used to bandits and outlaws far rougher around the edges than you. You seem like a gentleman compared to some of the company my father keeps."

"I take that as a compliment."

"I meant it as such." Dotty smiled up at him as she hurried to catch up with his long strides. "By the way, you owe me a cattleman's revolver. Preferably one with an improved grip.

I lost mine defending one of your stagecoaches, after all."

"You what?" Budd Mansfield whirled around and grabbed Dotty by the arm. "Please tell me you weren't stupid enough to engage the Blood Eagles."

Dotty yanked her arm out of his grasp and swatted him on the shoulder. "It is hardly my first time in a shootout, Mr. Mansfield! Besides, you should thank me. Your men never once returned fire and—"

"You do not know what you're talking about. Do not meddle in my affairs."

"Was I just supposed to *let them* rob the stagecoach?" Dotty huffed.

Budd Mansfield stormed off with her bag in tow, leaving her to hobble after him through the mud. He walked so fast that she had to run in order to match his speed.

"All right, Mr. Mansfield," she said. "I can see you are upset. Though I don't entirely know why, I feel obligated to ease your worries.

I did not intend to cause you any trouble. Please, allow me to make it up to you."

"How do you suppose you'll do that?" he asked as he arched his brow with a look of genuine curiosity. "You don't seem to make miracles, Miss Valentine. What sort of scheme could you possibly come up with that would fix my problems?"

"Let me accompany you on your next transport," Dotty offered. "I'm an excellent shot, and I'll fight any member of the Blood Eagles to the very end, if I must. They've killed more of my friends and family than I care to admit. I have as much to lose in this as you do."

"No."

"I insist."

Mr. Mansfield stopped at the end of the road that led to the estate. He handed Dotty her bag and turned to leave. "I don't care what you insist. Just leave me alone so I can go clean up the mess you've made."

Dotty blocked his way with her body. She brazenly placed a hand on the center of his chest. "Take me with you, Mr. Mansfield," she demanded. "Take me with you, or I will have to follow on my own, and who knows what sort of danger I might encounter."

He squinted his eyes. "You wouldn't be threatening me, would you?"

"I'm merely issuing a challenge," Dotty retorted. "If you think the Blood Eagles are your biggest problem, then you will soon learn I am a far more formidable opponent."

There was a stretch of silence between them.

Dotty felt the rise and fall of Budd Mansfield's chest as he breathed deeply through his nose, as if savoring her scent. The heat of his skin radiated through his buttoned shirt and vest.

She felt her cheeks flush and dropped her hand as if it had been burned. Dotty swallowed nervously, and Mr. Mansfield's eyes trailed down to her throat. "Do we have an accord, sir?" she stammered. "Or will you not rise to my challenge?"

***

The Old Mill

The iron door opened with a creak. Rip pulled his mask off and punched the nearest wall. He felt a jolt of pain, but it did little to dampen his anger. "Dotty Valentine!" Rip roared as his men entered the rundown shell of the old steel mill. "Find out why she's not in Nevada!"

Leroy stepped toward Rip with caution. "Who's Dotty Valentine, boss?"

Rip had almost forgotten that Pete, Charles, and Leroy hadn't been in his gang the last time he crossed paths with Dotty. Lord knew she was a spitfire and a better shot than even her father.

They had been lucky to have gotten away. Dotty could have taken out ten men on her own. Theodore Valentine had raised her right.

"Dotty Valentine is a vicious harpy," Rip told Leroy and the others. "There used to be a lot more of us. The Blood Eagles were fifty strong before Dotty led a group of raiders to our old hideout. I had thirteen men left when we arrived in California. Now there's only six of us."

"One woman did all that?" Charles scoffed. "I don't believe it."

It was Salazar who replied, "Dotty and her father's gang hunted us halfway across the territory before they finally lost our trail. We laid low in Timber for eight weeks. There was no use in rebuilding our numbers after that."

Rip remembered that day like it had just happened. He had heard the warning before three explosions took down their walls. Men flooded inside and killed without remorse. And Rip's men had deserved to spill every drop of blood that hit the ground. "We weren't robbing stagecoaches back then," he said, his voice raw with regret.

"Our gang was known for plundering homesteads. Men, women, and children died at our hands. Dotty's mother was among them."

A cold rush of dread filled Rip. He prayed to God—or anybody who would listen—that Dotty hadn't come to California in search of Budd Mansfield. Dotty and Mansfield were among the deadliest people Rip had ever met.

The thought of them teaming up to thwart him was nearly enough to shake his confidence. Nearly, but not quite.

Sal lowered himself into a nearby chair and tore the sleeve of his shirt off. Blood oozed from the hole in his shoulder. Pete retrieved the kit they often used to patch up bullet wounds. Rip frowned as screams filled the Old Mill as Pete removed the bullet and poured liquor over the hole to clean it. The whole sight made Rip feel rather ill.

He left them to it, not able to stomach much more. Besides, he had matters of great importance that required his attention. Rip reached into the loot bag before he tossed a stack of cash at Charles.

"Go to the surrounding settlements and hire some guns to stand guard. I've got something that needs doing in Sacramento," he commanded.

"Now?"

"Yes! This needs to be handled carefully," he shouted. "Now, go do as I say or it'll be you bleeding on the floor next." Rip stomped out of the room and into a makeshift bedchamber at the back of the main area of the factory.

He changed out of his all-black garb and into his favorite gray town suit. He stashed away his gear, headed out to Storm's hitch, and dragged himself back into the saddle.

"Clean yourselves up and go see what you can find out about the next job," he told Leroy and the others. "The stagecoach is carrying prospectors, so we need to know if there's gold on board."

The ride to Sacramento was filled with dark, ruthless thoughts of what Rip wanted to do to Dotty Valentine. He wanted her dead, that was for certain, but he also wanted her to suffer for the lives of the men he had lost.

Rip's gang was like his family. Every man in his employment was his brother in arms. Her actions on the road meant that she had once again endangered his brothers.

When he arrived in the city, Rip wasted no time in finding the Parlor Room. Lively music streamed out through the windows as he approached the long walkway. He strolled past the horses of drunken patrons and gamblers alike.

His gaze finally landed on a bright red door behind the bar. He paid the barman for his discretion and sauntered inside.

Madame Josephine sat at her vanity as she painted her lips a strawberry red. Her eyes glittered with mischief as she caught sight of him in the mirror. "Well, well, well," she purred. "Ripley Eagleson comes knockin' at my door.'

"I need your help again."

The madam turned in her seat and arched her brow. "You got some nerve after one of your boys carved up my Caroline," she hissed. "Poor girl can't work for me when she's got scars.

"I had to let her go, which is worse than if he had just killed her. No man wants spoiled goods, Ripley."

Rip nodded in understanding. He owed Madame Josephine a debt that couldn't be repaid. Working girls were more and more rare with each passing year. Most women were shouting about their rights in town squares, not working for a madam. "Dotty's in town."

"Sweet girl. Could make a fortune with me."

"She is not sweet from where I'm standing," he snapped. "She had blood on her hands already, and she just shot Sal. I need your girls to report to me if she's seen anywhere near Sacramento or Budd Mansfield."

Chapter 8

The Trail to Black Lake, California

The rain had stopped in the night—not that Budd had noticed. He had spent most of the evening wearing a hole in his bedchamber floor with all the pacing he had done. Dorothy Valentine had gotten under his skin quicker than any woman ever had in the past.

She angered him with her stubborn disposition. Miss Valentine hadn't acted like a lady should have, and that had made Budd react like a brute. Sheriff Dawson was right: Budd owed her an apology.

"Listen, Miss Valentine," he began. "The way I acted last night was out of line. I ain't usually so untoward with a lady, and I wouldn't want you to think ill of me. I shouldn't have—"

"Oh, don't be sorry. I was just starting to like you." Miss Valentine chuckled lightly and shot Budd a playful little wink. "Besides, I know I can bring out the worst in anyone. And, please, call me Dotty. Miss Valentine is a bit too formal."

Once again, Budd felt anger welling up inside of him. She should have just allowed him to make his apology so he wouldn't have lost his train of thought. But she had cut him off and babbled on about nonsense. Had she winked at him?

Budd scowled in confusion. Miss Valentine's behavior was strange indeed. While he was used to suggestive looks or blatant indifference to women, playfulness was something new entirely. "I think we should keep some formality between us," he replied.

Budd heard a snort and looked over at Blake Wright. The man seemed awfully amused by Budd's suffering.

Steven Wright, however, hadn't been able to keep his eyes off Dorothy Valentine since she climbed up onto the riding bench beside Budd that morning.

Something dark and ugly unfurled inside of Budd. He tore his gaze away from the brothers and back to the road as he snapped the reins. The stagecoach rattled along the sodden road, kicking up mud and stones.

Ivory trotted alongside the coach with three other riderless horses. The loyal mare never wandered off. She stayed close to Budd at all times.

"Wait," Miss Valentine said suddenly. She placed her hand over Budd's. "There are tracks up ahead. Someone has been down this way recently."

Budd pulled back on the reins and listened to the surrounding sounds. "Is that singing?" he asked in bewilderment. Budd raised his hand and signaled for the Wright brothers to investigate.

They climbed down the side of the stagecoach and onto their horses. Budd watched as they disappeared into the early morning fog.

Minutes ticked by.

Steven and Blake appeared with two men hogtied on their horses. "Claim jumpers," Blake hissed. "They were watching a few prospectors near the river. Had too much to drink and nearly shot my head off."

"Go north and cut across the flat lands so you ain't followed. Take them to Timber," Budd ordered. "Hand these scavengers over to the sheriff and then meet us in Black Lake."

There was hesitation in Budd's voice. He disliked the idea of being alone with Miss Valentine for any number of hours, much less the rest of the way to Black Lake. She sat much too close for his comfort.

"Don't worry, gentlemen," she told Steven and Blake with a warm smile. "We will get the passengers to Black Lake safe and sound."

That darkness inside of Budd was… envy? Miss Valentine was a beautiful woman, but he hadn't known her for even an entire day. There was no logical reason Budd could think of that would have explained why he felt such hideous jealousy.

His heart belonged to Rose Buchanan, and he doubted his feelings could ever change. Dorothy—or Dotty, Budd corrected—was the daughter of Theodore Valentine, and that made her off limits.

Budd tried his best to ignore her.

He kept his eyes on the horizon, scanning the distance for any sign of the bandits. Though the rain had stopped, the air was still damp. The stench of Oakhill Farm grew stronger as they rode by.

Cows lumbered through the grazing pastures. Dotty let out a giddy little squeal that almost brought a smile to his lips. A city girl like her must not have seen many animals growing up.

"Look, Mr. Mansfield!"

"I've seen cows before, Miss Valentine," he snorted. "If you think that's exciting, you might want to hang on to the bench when we pass some chickens."

She slapped his arm playfully and giggled, "Their tongues are as long as my arm!"

"Keep it down. We don't want folks knowing we're out on this road." Budd felt bad when the childlike excitement faded from her eyes. "We just don't know who the Blood Eagle gang has working for them."

"I... suppose you're right."

Budd cleared his throat and asked, "What are they like? The gang, I mean."

"They're different. Not like any bandits I've ever known." Dotty chewed on her bottom lip and tilted her head to the side. She looked him up and down without a single ounce of shame.

"They're more like you than my father."

"Oh? Is that right?"

"Their leader lives by a code," she explained. "He never takes off his mask, but I don't think I've ever seen him truly angry. There's a kindness to him that feels genuine.

I doubt he really wants to hurt people. Things just happen, I guess."

Dotty wasn't the first woman to have described the gang leader as kind. Nor did Budd suppose she would be the last. He was tired of folks believing criminals wanted more than just to watch the world crumble.

"But you've seen the others in the gang? You know their names," Budd supposed. "Can you tell me?"

"I only know two of them. Sal and Hector used to work for my father."

"Salazar Torez and Hector Vasquez?"

Dotty nodded her head. "They stole almost ten thousand dollars from my father and came here to California. I think they joined the Blood Eagles for protection."

***

Sacramento, California
Two days later

Rip wiped the sweat from his brow with a blood-stained rag. His bruised knuckles throbbed to the same rhythm as his heartbeat. The smell of damp soil and rusted steel filled his nostrils as he stood over Evan Farris.

"We've been at this for five hours," he sighed. "Eventually, you're goin' to give me what I want."

Evan Farris spat on the floor near Rip's boots. "I ain't some dejected criminal you can beat into submission."

"That badge can't hide the outlaw in you," Rip snickered. "Budd Mansfield might have given you a place in society, but now you wear the shackles of a civilized man. One mistake and they will lock you away with the rest of the dejected criminals."

The young deputy laughed before the pain in his battered body caused him to wince. Rip basked in the other man's pain, savored it like a fine wine. Evan Farris's swollen face flashed in the light of the dwindling oil lamp.

The darkness shielded Rip, wrapping around him like an old friend as he stroked the edge of his mask. He was half tempted to remove it just to see the stunned expression on the deputy's face.

"Tell me how Mansfield knew about the robbery," he ordered. "And tell me how he got those people to Black Lake without me knowin' about it."

Evan said nothing.

Rip pulled his arm back and launched another devastating punch right at the man's jaw. Evan collapsed against the wall. Ragged breaths bounced off the walls.

The deputy still had a bit of fight left in him. Evan launched himself at Rip, but Rip sidestepped the attack.

Rip watched as the other man crashed into the wall on the other side of the cellar. He kicked Evan to the floor and pressed his boot to his throat.

He enjoyed the way Evan's arms flailed, desperately trying to dislodge his foot. The pitiful little mewling that reached his ears was almost comical. He pressed his foot down a little harder and watched as Evan's eyes widened.

"Budd Mansfield, and I had a deal! He was supposed to look the other way while we robbed the coaches," Rip shouted.

"But he just had to work with that stupid rookie sheriff! And now you have to pay the price for his mistakes." He pulled out his revolver and cocked the hammer.

Guttural cries of fear echoed in the small room.

"Keep him quiet before the whole darn town figures out what's what," said Otis Greene, the owner of the gun shop.

Rip lifted his boot off Evan's throat and circled him like a vulture—no, like an eagle. "Your dear friend ain't as honorable as he'd like you to believe, Farris. He was working with outlaws, letting us take precious wealth from the people he was supposed to protect.

"Does that sound like a good man to you?"

Evan's hands gripped his throat as he coughed and gagged, trying to drag air into his lungs. Rip holstered his gun and kicked Evan one more time for good measure.

He then whistled joyfully beneath his mask as if he hadn't just beaten a man half to death. He pulled two hundred dollars out of his pocket and waved it in front of the shop owner.

"It's yours if you deliver our friend here to Budd Mansfield's address."

Otis barely hesitated as he snatched the money from Rip's fingers. "We got a deal."

Rip smiled at Otis. There was something he found almost endearing about folks who will sell their pride for a good price.

Rip patted Otis on the shoulder and then made his way up the cellar stairs. He opened the slender metal door and walked into the shop.

There was a pungent aroma of gun oil and black powder.

Rip helped himself to a few boxes of bullets on his way out the back door. As usual, the city was quiet at night. Only working girls and their drunk companions moved through the streets.

Rip moved along the edges of the buildings until he reached the hotel near the eatery. He entered through the back and greeted Sal outside their rented room.

Sal handed Rip a fresh set of clothes and a drink the moment he stepped through the door. "I think Mansfield is still out of town. He was not home or at the sheriff's office when I looked for him."

"Never mind that. How's your shoulder healing up?" Rip asked.

"Pain is not so bad anymore. Now it's been a few days. It's the itching I dislike." Sal adjusted the sling that kept his arm stable and sat down at a small tea table near the window.

"Is the deputy taken care of?"

"Yes. I think Budd Mansfield will learn his lesson. Kept Farris alive, though," Rip revealed. "I want to tear their little friendship apart—isolate Mansfield so he thinks there's no one he can turn to... and then I'll make him an offer."

"An offer for what?"

"To join us or die," Rip chuckled. "When Evan Farris tells the sheriff all about our deal with Budd Mansfield, he won't have a choice but to join us. Hell, he'll probably beg me to let him in."

There was an odd expression on Sal's face that made Rip uneasy.

"What?" he asked. "You don't think he'll join us?"

Sal shook his head. "I know what kind of man he is, señor. He is the sort of man who would rather die than join men like us."

Rip considered that for a moment. He had admitted to himself that Sal's argument was valid. But for a reason he could not fathom, the thought of Mansfield dead hadn't brought a smile to his face like it used to.

In fact, Rip knew Mansfield had been the best entertainment he'd had in the past five years. The routine of robbing stagecoaches had lost its excitement long ago, but the challenge Mansfield had injected had renewed Rip's fire. And it was a fire that burned brighter with each robbery.

Chapter 9

Black Lake, California

"What are you writing?" a voice said from over Dotty's shoulder. She craned her neck up at Budd Mansfield and smiled with a shrug. He was a rather inquisitive man, but Dotty liked that.

Most of the men she grew up with had seen little sense in questioning her father. Dotty just knew Budd Mansfield was different. He wouldn't have backed down from her father or any of his men.

"It's a journal," she replied. "I like to write."

He squinted down at the page and cocked his head to the side like a hunting dog listening for its master's whistle.

"You like to write about what? About how you told the innkeeper's wife we were married? Or how you stole my pistol and strapped it to your leg the second I took my eyes off you?"

Dotty bit the inside of her cheek as she fought to keep her giggle at bay. When she finally stifled her laughter, she answered, "I write about all of my experiences. The good and the bad. I find it keeps me honest, and it allows me to understand things.

And besides, I think the innkeeper's wife was quite tickled by the idea of us being married after she saw just how red your face—"

"I don't blush."

"Of course not." Dotty finally lost the battle, and a bout of laughter burst from her lips. She smacked her hand over her mouth, but her shoulders still shook with mirth. "I apologize, Mr. Mansfield. How rude of me. You must think I'm a wild woman."

He stomped over to the other side of the room. "I think nothing of you, Miss Valentine. All I know is that you have done nothing to prove you can be trusted."

"I told you about the attack." She closed the journal and tucked it back into her bag. "And I am borrowing your pistol until I can replace my revolver."

"The one you used to shoot a member of the Blood Eagle gang," he grumbled irritably.

Dotty had apologized several times for complicating whatever it was he had planned for the gang, but he seemed reluctant to forgive her. "How can I prove myself in your eyes?"

Budd Mansfield finally met Dotty's gaze. "You told me why you came to California, but I said I can't help you.

All I need is for you to go back to wherever you came from and stay away from the Blood Eagles. I have this under control."

"Do you really expect me to believe that?" Dotty asked boldly. "People around Sacramento know all you've done is get people killed." She hated herself the moment the words left her lips.

Dotty knew her words had cut Budd Mansfield right to the bone, and the pain in his expression nearly brought a tear to her eye. "I'm sorry."

"You want to know why I'm so angry?"

Dotty walked over to him and placed her hand gently on his arm. "Please."

"I'm angry because I don't know what to do anymore," he said. "People are losing faith in me because this gang is still out there.

Hell, I've lost faith in myself."

"What's holding you back?"

"They ambushed me," Budd replied. "They beat me, and they told me to ignore the robberies. Said they'd stop killing folks if I let them take the money. I was weak."

That... explained a lot. Dotty curled her fingers around his bicep and stared into the oceans of his eyes. "You did the right thing," she said.

"You weren't weak, Mr. Mansfield. I know how this gang works. I know they break you down until there's nothing left. You traded your honor to save lives, and it was all you thought you had, but you're wrong."

"Yeah? What else am I holding on to, then?"

"I don't know. Maybe your courage? Your determination to make things right? All I know for sure is this isn't over.

"They haven't won until we're both dead and gone." Dotty lowered her hand and walked over to the window. She pushed open the shutters, letting in the fresh summer breeze.

"You might not want me here, but I feel like God brought me to California to help you... or maybe to save you from yourself."

Wagons rolled on by as children played in the street. Dotty waved at the young ones who had spied her in the second-story window of the inn. She had felt invisible at her father's side for years.

In California she felt seen. With Budd Mansfield, she felt… stirrings in her heart that she couldn't fathom. There was an energy about the man that put Dotty on edge, made her misbehave in ways she never even considered back home.

She had brazenly commandeered his weapon and purposely goaded him into confrontation without a single ounce of guilt. Budd Mansfield made her recklessly brave.

"You said you can't help my father, and I understand why. But I wish to stay with you, Mr. Mansfield. I want to help you bring the Blood Eagle gang to justice, and I want to do so as equals." Dotty peered over at him and gasped at the sight of his wounded expression.

She left her place at the window and inched her way closer to him once more.

Budd lifted his hand to keep her at bay, but she stepped into his corner of safety.

"Did I say something wrong, Mr. Mansfield?" Dotty asked.

"You should know… I'm… uhh… that I'm in love with someone," he whispered. "Whatever you might feel toward me will pass. It always does.

My heart belongs to someone else—to someone who isn't mine to love."

"Rose Buchanan."

"H-how did you know?"

"I might have suspected." Dotty chuckled, but it was a hollow sound, devoid of any genuine joy. "But my reason for staying isn't this… vibration… between us.

"My reason for staying is the same as yours. I stay because I have to."

***

Sacramento, California

Budd pulled the stagecoach into the stables and exhaled slowly as Dotty left. The woman was an enigma to a man like him. No woman had ever treated him as if he was worth more than a few stolen moments or as if their interest in him went beyond his skills as a manhunter.

In his line of work, fleeting romances were quite common, but Budd had no intention of further complicating his life. He had enough problems.

So instead of following Dotty to the sheriff's office, Budd headed home for the night. The ride back to the city had seemed much longer with the silence that had wedged its way between them.

Even Blake and Steven Wright hadn't said more than a few awkward phrases along the way. Dotty had been plotting quietly to herself since they left the inn. Whatever she had planned, Budd hoped it wasn't dangerous.

He cut through the alleyways, squeezing between the buildings until his home came into view. Budd avoided all the main roads in the city and kept his head down as he walked.

Just as he rounded the corner, Budd heard heavy footfalls behind him. He spun around quickly, ready to defend himself if necessary, but he let down his guard when he saw Blake Wright. "What is it?" Budd asked. "Why are you sneaking up behind me?"

"I wasn't sneakin' up behind anybody. I just came to let you know Evan is in the infirmary. Doc says he doesn't know how long he'll be able to stay conscious, and Evan is askin' for you."

Blake's tone gave away just how worried the man was. In fact, Budd would have wagered Blake was closer to Evan than he was to his own brother.

Nothing—not even Dotty Valentine or Rose Buchanan—could have stopped Budd from reaching the infirmary. He dropped his bags on the porch and followed Blake.

They ran straight down the dirt road, dodging wagons and stagecoaches. Drivers shouted for them to get out of the way. Mothers grabbed their children, and folks looked on with curiosity.

Budd saw and heard nothing other than the sound of his boots as they pounded against the ground.

He had lost friends before, either to the hard life of the West or to foolishness, but Budd refused to let Evan be another one of those losses.

Blake led him right to Evan's bed when they arrived. The poor man was covered in bruises and dry, crusted blood.

"What happened to him?" Budd asked no one in particular.

Steven handed Budd an ace of spades that was splattered with even more blood. "That was pinned to his chest with a throwing knife."

Budd crushed the card in his fist. He shook with rage as he stepped to the side of Evan's bed. Evan trembled with each breath, grimacing in pain. Budd grabbed his friend's hand in his and squeezed. "I'm here."

"He said…" Evan slurred through swollen lips. "He said you made a deal with them. T-that you let them rob the coaches."

Budd felt as if the world tilted. His gut clenched tightly as he glanced up and locked eyes with Sheriff Dawson. The fury he saw in the lawman's eyes rivaled his own.

The problem was that Sheriff Dawson's anger was aimed directly at Budd. "I had to," Budd sighed. "They're planning something big, and we can't afford to lose more people."

"There's always a choice," argued Sheriff Dawson.

"And I saved the people rather than the money." Budd turned his gaze back to Evan. "Helping the passengers get to Black Lake is what caused this. The gang must think I broke our arrangement. I'm sorry, Evan. I never meant for this to happen."

Evan's eyes fluttered until they closed slowly.

The doctor pulled Budd away from the bed and ushered all of them out of the infirmary. Sheriff Dawson was on him the instant they were outside.

Budd's back hit the wall in the blink of an eye, but he hadn't put up a fight.

"If you start this," he growled. "You better be ready to finish it. Because I will not take a beating without defending myself, Sheriff.

"Do you really think so little of me?"

Sheriff Dawson released Budd with a sneer. "Mr. Thayer will hear about this."

"Let me tell him myself," Budd said. "He deserves to hear the truth from me."

"Yeah? And what exactly is the truth?"

Budd shut his eyes for a moment and breathed deeply. He stood up straight and adjusted his jacket as he answered, "I was in a tough situation without many options. We were piling up bodies and getting no closer to putting the men responsible behind bars."

"So you made a deal with the devil?" Dawson asked.

"No, I saved as many lives as I could while I came up with a better plan." He left Blake, Steven, and Sheriff Dawson at the infirmary and went home.

Dotty Valentine sat on the front porch with her bag in her lap. Her shoulders were slumped, and he could have sworn he saw tears in her eyes.

"May I stay with you for a little while?" she sniffled.

"I can't deal with this right now, Dotty… My friend, Evan, he's hurt real bad." Budd cleared his throat and picked up his bags from the porch. He unlocked the front door, kicked it open, and lumbered inside without a glance in her direction.

"Let me make you some coffee." Dotty set her bag on the sofa and disappeared into the kitchen. She rummaged around the cupboards until she found the kettle. "Sit down and tell me what happened. Maybe I can help."

Chapter 10

Sacramento, California

A knock on the door summoned Rip from his deep sleep. He reached for the revolver beneath his pillow and eased out of bed. The floorboards creaked outside the door as he silently moved closer. A second knock came. He turned the doorknob and pulled it open just a hair.

Sheriff Dawson greeted him with a frown. "You're back in town," the lawman said. "After your sister disappeared, I never thought you would return."

"I took her somewhere safe so that she can properly mourn her husband." Rip set his revolver on the wardrobe and allowed Sheriff Dawson entrance. "What can I do for you at this hour, Sheriff? I thought you had your hands full with this gang robbing stagecoaches."

"I need a favor, Reginald."

"Naturally," he said with a smile. "But I'm in no position to offer much."

Dawson took a seat at the end of the bed and removed his hat. "Budd Mansfield got into some trouble. His partner was beaten and stabbed because of it.

Now, I need someone with influence—someone like you with the support of the people in this city—to talk to the mayor. Budd Mansfield can't handle this on his own, and I was a fool to think otherwise."

"You want to bring in a marshal?"

Sheriff Dawson nodded his head subtly. "We need help."

Rip smiled even as he clenched his jaw. He walked over to the tray near his bed and poured himself a drink. A U.S. Marshal was bad news for the gang.

There weren't many in the region who would have been willing to take a bribe from a group of outlaws. Rip thought carefully for a second. "Maybe what you need is to give Budd Mansfield another chance," he offered. "He's human. Humans make mistakes."

"Mansfield made a deal with the gang."

"I'm sure he thought it was the best decision," Rip said with a careful, even tone to not show his hand. "Give him another chance to set this right."

Sheriff Dawson was quiet for a moment. He scratched at his jaw and bounced his leg nervously. "He managed to get the passengers to Black Lake safely. Perhaps he is coming up with a new plan to stop the gang."

"I thought the roads were being watched by the outlaws."

"They are," Dawson answered. "Budd Mansfield knew about a road that wasn't on any of the recent maps of Sacramento Valley. He used it to get the stagecoach to safety while the gang was on a different road."

Rip slammed his glass onto the tray. The amber liquid sloshed over the rim of the crystal. He wiped his hands on a nearby rag. "Clumsy hands," he explained as he saw the look on the sheriff's face. "But it sounds to me like Budd Mansfield has all this under control. What happened to his friend is a tragedy, I'm sure, but give the man a chance."

He poured Sheriff Dawson a drink, and they talked well into the early hours of the morning. The lawman was full as a tick by the time Rip got the courage to ask about the road Mansfield had used.

Though most of what the sheriff had said was gibberish, Rip made out Calligan Road and Oakhill Farm amid the drunken man's rambling. He wrote down every little detail he could before the sun rose over the city. When Sheriff Dawson fell unconscious, Rip grabbed his jacket and hurried out the door.

The stableboy had Storm saddled and ready within the hour. Rip rode east toward Yosemite Valley and beyond the forest that scattered over the landscape. He followed a long forgotten path toward the Old Mill.

There, nestled in the mountainous terrain, was his fortress. Hours upon hours of riding in the saddle had felt like a single second.

Leroy pushed open the gate when he arrived, and Jorge was waiting to take Storm. Rip lowered himself from the saddle onto numb legs. He took a moment and caught his breath before he walked into the factory. His footsteps echoed in the cavernous room as he approached his usual seat. The men gathered instinctively, circling the table with expectant expressions on their faces.

"We got ourselves a problem," he said roughly. "Sheriff Dawson wants me to talk to the mayor so he can request the help of a U.S. Marshal."

Distasteful curses filled the air.

Rip glared at his men and continued, "I think I convinced him not to, but we still need to have our guard up. Budd

Mansfield and a couple of deputies is one thing, but a marshal... a marshal could find this place and call in the cavalry."

"What do we do?" Hector asked.

"Keep our heads down." Rip took a cigar from the table, clenched it between his teeth, and lit the end with a match. "No more saloons, no more girls, and no more fights. I mean it. We work a job, and then we lie low."

"That ain't fair!" Charles shouted. "I got a poker game comin' up."

Rip grabbed the pistol from Leroy's holder and shot the table a hair's breadth away from Charles's hand. The outlaw jumped back from the table and looked at Rip as if he had gone mad. Rip took a long drag on his cigar and exhaled the thick smoke through his nostrils. "We work a job and we lie low. Anyone who has trouble understanding that can discuss it with me in private."

No one argued.

One by one, the outlaws left the room, keeping their eyes on Rip as if they expected him to snap and shoot them in the back. He was a lot of things, but he was no coward.

Ripley Eagleson looked a man in the eyes as he pulled the trigger. That was the difference between him and an outlaw.

***

Sacramento, California

Hot, damp air fluttered the curtains. Dotty sat at the table across from Budd Mansfield as she steeped her coffee. Her eyes took in the sight of his slumped shoulders and defeated expression. The smell of sweat and horse stuck to the two of them, but neither was bothered. Dotty figured he would talk when he was ready.

"I didn't have many friends when I came here," he revealed. "Evan and I just sort of... connected. He survived the worst tragedy a man could ever face, yet he found it easy to smile.

"Even after we avenged the death of his wife and child, he stuck by me."

Dotty reached across the table and rested her hand upon Budd's. He stroked the inside of her wrist with the pad of his thumb. Dotty stared down at their entwined hands and felt the strength of him. In all her life, Dotty had never felt the sort of companionship Budd described.

His bond with Evan Farris was unlike anything Dotty had shared with anyone. "I know how it feels to live your life thinking that being alone is all you deserve," she whispered. "But Evan is still alive, Mr. Mansfield. Do not give up hope. He will prevail."

There was a knock at the door. Both of them reached for their guns. Dotty checked the backdoor while Budd headed toward the front.

She looked out into the darkness and saw a wagon near the feeding troughs. Voices carried through the house, and Dotty's heart dropped. Rose and Douglas Buchanan stood in the doorway.

"Dorothy," Rose said plainly. "I apologize for the way I had treated you. You are the daughter of my husband's business associate, so I should not have held your... reputation against you so harshly."

Dotty crossed her arms and cocked her hip to the side. "My reputation is intact," she replied. "It is your perception of me that is askew, Mrs. Buchanan.

Being seen in the company of Budd Mansfield should not have—"

Budd's head whipped toward Rose and Douglas Buchanan. Dotty saw such heartache in his eyes. Despite whatever history the three of them shared—Budd Mansfield's heart was in the palm of Rose's hand.

"Now, wait one minute! Being seen with me supposedly tainted her reputation?"

Rose had the nerve to look embarrassed for a split second before her mask of propriety slid back into place. "I meant no offense," Rose said.

"She is unmarried, and you are… well, you are still a mystery to the people of this city. People who talk."

Dotty moved to stand between them and lowered her arms. "Never mind all this. Why have you come?"

Douglas spoke in his wife's stead. He placed a hand gently upon her shoulder and answered, "Our intentions were pure, honestly. We came to invite you back into our home, and we extend our condolences to our dear friend Budd. It must be dreadful to lose a partner."

"Friend?" Dotty looked over her shoulder at the tall man who looked over her.

Budd's frown deepened. Dotty had suspected some sort of acquaintanceship, but friends were something different entirely. They treated him with the same cold detachment they had treated her with.

It definitely was not the way one treated a friend.

"I'm afraid my reputation will have to take another blow," Dotty said. "I will stay here for the rest of my time in Sacramento. Mr. Mansfield and I are working together to help the stagecoach company."

Something odd flashed in Rose's eyes. Dotty wasn't sure what it was, but she pasted a smile upon her face and walked their uninvited guests back out the door.

She wished them a good evening before closing the door.

Dotty rested her forehead on the wooden frame to catch her breath. "How are you friends with them? They seem terribly dull."

"I—it's a long story."

"Well, it's a long night," she chuckled. "And I have some dusting to do in that room upstairs before I unpack my things."

"Rose is right, you know. People will think the worst of us." Budd placed his hat on the hook beside the door and toed off his boots. "It's improper."

"You said 'to hell with the law' at the sheriff's office the day I arrived," she reminded him. "So I say to hell with what's proper. Theodore is my father.

"I've camped in the wilderness with outlaws, fought off dozens of bandits, and lived to tell the story. I'll survive the gossip."

Dotty saw a slight smile tug at the corner of his lips. She patted him on the arm and returned to the kitchen.

Two cups of cold coffee sat on the table, along with some dry biscuits. She tidied everything up as he returned to his seat.

"We were at the orphanage together," he blurted. "Me, Douglas, and Rose were the best of friends. Just reckless kids."

"What changed?"

"I changed," he replied. "Started getting into trouble. Learned to fight and use a gun. A man named James White saw potential in me—gave me a job with the Pinkertons. I was nothing more than their hunting dog. I hurt people. Killed some too."

Dotty's blood ran cold. "You thought they were outlaws."

"I never cared to ask," Budd explained. "I even got Douglas involved. A wealthy family adopted Rose, and she saw me for who I really was... a monster."

"You aren't a monster," Dotty insisted. "I've seen how much you care for others. I know the sacrifices you've made to help this city." She pulled him up out of the chair and removed his filthy jacket. A bit of dirt crumbled onto his shirt, and she brushed it away with her hand.

Budd seemed to ignore her. "Rose's family wanted to marry her off to some solicitor who was known for being cruel to women.

"She asked us for help. I was content with my life, and I had no time for her problems. Douglas wanted out, so he and Rose eloped. He married the woman I loved—the woman who I love."

Chapter 11

Black Lake, California

Gunfire rained down outside of Holmes Bank.

"Stand down, gringos!"

Ten men surrounded Salazar Torez. The outlaw had his back to the bank doors and a smile on his face. He held his gun in one hand and a bag of money in the other. His shoulders burned from the effort it took to carry the loot, but he looked forward to spending it. If, of course, he got out of Black Lake alive.

"This is Sheriff Baker! You have ten seconds to lower your gun, or else we will shoot you dead. This is your last warning!"

"You will not take me back to the prison, amigo," Sal snorted. "And I will not die without a fight. I'll take some of you with me to the grave if I have to."

"Ain't no need for things to come to that, son. We've lost a lot of good men to this mess already today." The sheriff stepped out from behind his cover, and the deputies lowered their weapons. "What's your name?"

"My name is Salazar Torez," he chuckled.

The sheriff's expression hardened. "Torez, eh? I heard of you."

"Good. Because it will be the name people whisper in the dark, the one they will say when they retell the story of how you died, amigo."

Three lawmen changed positions, closing in on Sal. He shot the first deputy who appeared on his right, and the sheriff charged.

Sal hid behind one of the bank's pillars as the deputies fired right at him. Bullets popped holes into the walls of the bank. Sal counted to ten before he lunged from behind the pillar and tackled the sheriff.

They crashed to the ground. Sal pushed the lawman's gun away and rammed his knee into the sheriff's ribs. He punched him again and again until his knuckles ached. The sheriff curled into a ball and coughed harshly.

Sal held his gun to the lawman's head. "Stand down," he shouted to the deputies. "Or I will kill him! I mean it!"

The deputies laid their firearms down.

Sal stood up and tossed his head back with manic laughter. "You fool thought you could kill me. I have killed gringos much stronger than you."

He cursed in Spanish as the sheriff kicked him in the back of the knees. Sal hit the pillar so hard that he sucked in a sharp breath. His chest clenched painfully as his gun discharged by accident.

Lawmen scattered in search of cover. Sal then raised his gun and fired blindly at the sheriff. He peered around the corner and dashed across the road. His boots hit the wooden planks of the sidewalk with loud thuds just before he threw himself through the general store window.

Glass sprayed everywhere. Bullets pelted the shop.

Sal rolled to the side and reloaded his pistol with deft fingers. He counted each round before he fired through the broken window. Sweat poured into his eyes.

A cloud of white filled the air as sacks of flour exploded. Powder fell to the floor like snow. Gunshots roared like an untamed beast in a cage. And through the dust and chaos, he caught movement out of the corner of his eye.

The shop owner had made a break for the back door. There was a way out.

Sal climbed to his feet and limped across the room. He shoved the man into the line of fire and leaped out of the rear exit.

His eyes scanned his surroundings until they landed on a wind-broken, flea-ridden horse near a mercantile cart. He set the bag of money down long enough to unhook the workhorse from the cart's harness. He then flung himself onto the horse's back with his loot in hand. And as Sal rode away from the sound of gunshots, the lawmen gave chase.

Sunlight burned his eyes, but he kept riding. The sound of hooves drew closer as the lawmen pulled up beside him with their guns aimed at his head.

Sal spurred the horse, yanking the stubborn mount from side to side as he dodged the bullets. He cut off the nearest deputy and jumped onto the lawman. The deputy tumbled from the saddle and was trampled by another rider. Sal laughed once more as he veered off the main road toward a path that circled around the town and headed right toward the Mojave Desert.

He got the lawman's horse under control, with a few demanding tugs on the reins. The path narrowed before it came to a fork. One direction led to a quarry, and the other led deeper into the desert.

Sal chose the desert path without a second thought. It was a path he knew the lawmen couldn't follow. Outlaws, Indians, and claim jumpers were just a few of the many reasons lawmen avoided the desert trails.

But the vast, lawless landscape of the Mojave was the perfect refuge for men like Sal.

Ten miles outside of Black Lake was a hidden cache. A cache just inside of a cave that served as a hideout in case the gang ran into trouble.

Sal's brief hiccup at the bank would anger Rip, so he had no choice but to hunker down at the cave. He rode as far away from civilization as possible, pushing the lawman's horse to a breakneck speed.

The cave came into sight, along with the wagon that Sal and Charles had stashed before they were arrested.

They filled the wagon with gun crates and ammunition. Sal looked back on the day they cleaned out a gun shop as if it was a fond memory. After all, it was all they had left from the old days when their numbers had been much greater.

But as Rip's chosen leader, Sal supposed there was time to reestablish the gang's dominance over the region. They needed more men and more money. Sal knew just where to find both.

He looked down at the bag of cash in his hand as he slowed the horse. It was just enough to pay off some bounties and get some of his old friends back into California. Men, he knew who weren't afraid to get their hands dirty.

***

Sacramento, California

Budd sat beside Evan with his head hung low and eyes bloodshot. He stared at his unconscious friend with a heavy heart. Evan hadn't deserved such a horrible act of cruelty.

Every couple of minutes, Budd stuck his finger under Evan's nose just to remind himself Evan had survived. The bruised, hollowed cheeks and sunken eyes barely resembled the man Budd had come to know by his insufferably cunning grin.

He rested his hand on the bed and lowered his voice to a whisper. "I... I ain't too sure if you can hear me, partner. I just wanted to let you know that I won't let you down."

"He can hear you," a voice said from over Budd's shoulder. To his surprise, Rose Buchanan stood in the doorway of Evan's room. She smiled sadly as her gaze moved from Budd to Evan. "My mother was like this for a year before she woke up. When she finally came to, she would tell me stories about God and how she heard my voice calling to her."

Budd felt a bit comforted by Rose's words, but he couldn't imagine an entire year without Evan Farris and his childish antics. "What are you doing here, Rose?"

"I just wanted to apologize," she replied. "I have not been kind to you since we arrived in Sacramento. Things are more complicated than I expected."

"Complicated, how?"

Tears glistened in Rose's eyes. "My reasons for coming here were pure in the beginning. I never want to be unfaithful to my husband, but I... I cannot stop thinking about you, Budd. That's why I wrote to you all these years… because it broke my heart when you let me marry Douglas. I wanted to marry you."

Budd's eyes widened as he stood up from the chair. He wasn't prepared for a conversation of such magnitude. "This ain't the time, Rose," Budd whispered. "And this certainly should be a conversation you have with Douglas."

Rose stepped toward Budd, but he shuffled back. Hurt sparked fiercely in her watery gaze.

"I've always loved you, Budd Mansfield. Even when I didn't have the courage to tell you. But when I saw you the other night with Dorothy Valentine…"

Oh, Budd thought. "You saw me with Dotty and thought we were together?"

"Aren't you?" Rose asked. "You seemed so… familiar with one another."

Budd shook his head. "We're working together. Her father knows the men I'm after, and she helps the sheriff and I save the stagecoach company."

Rose whipped away her tears and said, "Then, there is still hope for us. I can leave Douglas, and you and I can run away together—"

Budd grabbed Rose by the arms and pulled her closer, even as he was careful not to look too deeply into her eyes. "Listen to me, Rose. You love Douglas.

"On Sundays after church, you host dinner parties in your fancy houses. You've never approved of the way I live my life. It was the right thing to marry him. Don't throw all that away just because you saw me with someone."

"What are you saying, Budd?"

"I'm saying it's time that I move on," he explained. "I can't keep loving you from afar, knowing you're with him.

"You insult me to my face and then write the sweetest letters I've ever read, asking me if I'll still love you when we're old. I'm not someone you can manipulate and push aside whenever you feel like it. I'm done."

"No! Don't do this." Rose reached up and cupped Budd's cheek.

He lowered her hand and stepped away from her again. "You can't just tell me you want to run away and expect I'll follow. I've never told you how I feel, but I always suspected you knew deep down I was in love with you. But I'm tired, Rose."

"Rose?" Douglas's voice cut through their moment like a cannon blast as he called for his wife. Rose jumped away from Budd and tidied herself up before she ran out the door.

Budd watched her walk out without a single regret. He had done the right thing, no matter how hard it had been. There was a part of him that was still human, he supposed. A part that wasn't as selfish and heartless as he thought.

"You are a fool," Evan said in a raspy voice.

Budd hurried over to the bed and kneeled beside his friend. "But I'm a selfless fool."

Evan snorted. His lips curled into something Budd assumed was a smile. "You should have gotten out of here when you had the chance."

"And leave you here to clean up this mess?" Budd asked. "Not a chance."

Evan's eyes rolled into the back of his head as he fell in and out of consciousness. His labored breaths grew shallower with each second that passed. Evan reached out and grabbed onto Budd's hand. "Don't... let them win," he whispered. "Don't let the gang win."

"You got it, partner." Budd held his breath as Evan passed out. He stood up and left the room.

A nurse smiled over at him as he wandered the hall.

He opened his satchel, pulled out some cash, and handed it to the young woman. "This is for the meds. Give him something to take the edge off. I'll be back tomorrow."

"I'm sure he'll appreciate it, Mr. Mansfield." She hurried off to tend to Evan's needs.

Budd plopped his hat on and tugged it lower onto his forehead, shielding his eyes from the sun. Dotty Valentine waited just outside the infirmary with her knife in hand.

She scraped under her nails with the serrated tip, glaring at the folks who passed by with judgmental expressions on their faces. But a smile bloomed on her lips when she spotted him as he stepped over the threshold.

"I saw Rose and Douglas," Dotty said. "I assume you finally told her how you feel."

"Actually... she told me I was the one she wanted to marry."

The utter shock in Dotty's eyes would have been hilarious if not for the dark edge he saw in their depths. She seemed genuinely upset on his behalf. "What sort of woman—you know what?

"Never mind. I won't sit here and prattle on about self-respect and all that. How'd you take the news?"

"I was happy at first," he admitted. "And then I saw it for what it was."

"It'll save you the heartache later, trust me." Dotty picked up her bag and carried it over to the stagecoach.

"But now that Rose Buchanan has been firmly put in her place, let's get to work guarding this coach."

Chapter 12

Black Lake, California

Sunlight spilled into the saloon as Ripley Eagleson pushed through the swinging doors. He walked with the confidence and swagger of a man who knew he was untouchable. The server slid a drink across the bar as he passed, and Rip caught the glass in one fluid motion. Girls preened like a flock of birds, their eyes staring after him with lecherous intent. But Rip kept his steely eyes trained on the table near the back rooms.

Pete, Leroy, Hector, and Charles greeted him with fear and respect in equal measure. Rip shook each of their hands and turned his attention to Salazar as he took his seat at the table. Salazar avoided Rip's gaze.

Rip took a drink from his glass and set it on the table. "When I walk into a room and one of my men has the audacity to disrespect me," he growled, "I get furious. And when I am angry, I'm violent. Ain't that right, Sal?"

Salazar turned his head toward Rip. "Yes, boss?"

"You were here in town last week, weren't you?" he asked. "I believe my exact instructions were for you to listen for any sign of Budd Mansfield. Is that correct?"

"Sí."

"And you were in town at the same time that bank was robbed." Rip reached down and unsheathed the knife from his boot. "Was it you who robbed it?"

"Listen, boss, it was not my fault," Sal stammered. "We needed money to hire men to help us with this. There are six guards riding with the stagecoaches now, and they all have guns. I did not want our next job to end badly."

"We do not rob banks. Because when a bandit robs a bank, he's robbing the people. And we do not rob people. We rob the stagecoach company because the insurance covers any losses, so the only one paying for our crimes is Pratt Dempcy." Rip flipped the knife with a flourish and then buried the blade into the top of Salazar's hand. He twisted the blade and pulled it out with a quick jerk.

Sal fell out of his chair, grasping his injured hand. Blood painted the table red.

Rip snapped his fingers and a server brought over a rag. He held the rag over Sal's ravaged hand. "I wanted you to do one thing, and that was to lie low," Rip sighed. "I hope you got some good money."

"Seven thousand."

Rip whistled through his teeth at the impressive score. "So you walked in and just took the money? Didn't I teach you better than that?"

"I stabbed the guard and made the manager get the cash from the safe and made sure to draw the Royal Heart sign on the wall before I left."

"Then you shot up half the town on your way out. Yeah, I know the rest. Sheriff Baker could hardly wait to chew my ear off over what you did. What did you do with the money?

And if you say you spent it on that pretty little thing upstairs, I'll cut this hand off and feed it to the dogs out back." Rip squeezed Sal's hand to get his point across.

Sal nodded his head toward a table of rough-looking degenerates. "I paid for their bounties. Now they want to help the Blood Eagle gang."

There was a flashing moment of anger that had coursed through Rip. He was ready to stab Sal again before a brilliant idea came to him. "Go over there and tell our new friends they got a job if they want it," he said. "You're going to teach them how to rob stagecoaches like real outlaws."

"What about us?" Charles inquired.

"I have big plans for you." Rip dropped the rag and Sal's hand and picked up his drink. He brought the glass to his lips and sipped the decadent liquid inside. "But first I want to discuss my chat with Sheriff Dawson."

Leroy scoffed dismissively. "He ain't nothin' more than a boy dressed up in his papa's clothes. Plenty of the other sheriffs know we're good to keep around."

"Well, that boy is ready to call in a marshal if we're not careful," Rip said. "Dawson is the only sheriff who will not accept a bribe. That means masks up and boots down, gentlemen. Sacramento is now on high alert thanks to the stunt Sal pulled here in Black Lake." Rip wiped his hand clean on Sal's sleeve.

Charles reached over and smacked Sal on the head. "I'll stay with him and make sure he doesn't get into trouble. We'll be at the cache if you need us."

"And then I'll need you to get some regular clothes for the five of you," Rip ordered. "You and Leroy will be passengers on the next job. Pete and Hector will dress as guards. Those five hooligans will ride with Sal until I say otherwise."

Leroy slammed his beer down. "Is Sal gettin' his own crew?"

"Sit down, Leroy," Rip said calmly.

"Not until you tell me why he gets to lead his own crew. Just don't seem fair."

Rip grabbed Leroy by the back of his neck and pulled him closer. "Do you think I care about fairness?" he whispered into Leroy's ear. "I care about money. And if you want your family to stay under my protection, then I suggest you shut your mouth and sit down."

Leroy nodded stiffly and sat back down in his chair. "So we dress up like fools and infiltrate the stagecoach. What then? Ain't like Pratt Dempcy are just goin' to let us do it."

The table went quiet as the men looked at Rip expectantly.

Rip swirled his finger around the rim of his glass as he glared at his men with a slight frown. "I'm disappointed that I even have to say this… but we have to get Pete and Hector hired by the stagecoach company. they will use disguises and fake names so no one recognizes them, but once they're on the inside, the rest will go smoothly. Mr. Thayer is a gullible fool. He'll fall for the scheme."

***

Calligan Road
Sacramento Valley, California

The driver and the shotgun rode up front while Budd rode in the back with the three gentlemen they picked up in Timber. And so far, all had been quiet, aside from the churning of the wheels and the sound of hooves. None of the men in the stagecoach seemed keen on conversation. Two of the three had their noses in the pages of a newspaper while the other man napped. Budd simply stared out the window as he breathed in the fresh air.

He wasn't sure why the isolation of Calligan Road eased his spirit so much. There was just something about the way the Mojave's vast desert dwarfed the rest of the landscape that filled him with a sense of freedom. He reckoned the road was safe enough that he could accompany the coach without Dotty or the Wright brothers by his side. After all, Budd wouldn't have been able to appreciate the sights of nature if he hadn't gone alone with the stagecoach.

The problem was that he had run out of things to think about that weren't Buchanan. She had shaken up his world with just a few words. How long had she loved him? Were her feelings for him true, or were they just a ploy to escape her mundane life? Budd wasn't sure about much lately. As the stagecoach came around the bend, Budd was certain he saw dark shadows near the ruins of an old mining camp. He reached for his gun, and the gentlemen across from him glanced up from their newspapers.

"Stay down," he told them. "I think I saw something up ahead."

The third man awakened from his nap at the sound of Budd's rough voice. Budd slid across the seat and moved closer to the window. He tipped his hat down and peered beneath the brim as the shadows moved. The driver stopped suddenly, most likely having sensed something was wrong.

Budd pounded on the roof of the stagecoach when he saw a familiar horse. The Blood Eagles. "Move!" Budd shouted to the driver.

The stagecoach surged down Calligan Road. Budd stopped the other men as they reached for their own firearms. He shook his head and leaned out of the window. Six riders in black masks came up beside the coach. Dust stung Budd's eyes as he fought to see the bandits through the cloud of dirt that bellowed from the wheels. Sunlight glinted off the end of a rifle. Budd grabbed the third man and threw him to the floor of the stagecoach before he draped his larger frame over the man. A gunshot knocked the door clean off the hinges.

The stagecoach rocked from the force of the blast and Budd went flying out the cabin. He hit the ground hard. Air exploded from his lungs as he rolled across the dirt road to avoid being trampled. Budd pounded his fist against his chest until he was able to draw breath. Dry, ragged coughs rattled his bones. Black spots danced in his vision, and the world seemed to have tilted on its side. Nausea bubbled up, and there was a foul taste on his tongue.

Budd looked around and saw nothing but a desert. He searched for the road in a mad scramble. His hands touched the ground, prodding for horse tracks or drag marks from the wheels. There was nothing. He must have been thrown further than he thought, then passed out. The unforgiving sun pelted him with waves of heat. Sweat dripped down his spine and fell to the ground with a hiss of steam.

Hot stones burned his palms as he crawled slowly over to a small cluster of large rocks. Budd removed the rifle from his back and checked his satchel for ammunition. There wasn't much, but he had to make do in case the gang circled back. Armed with only one rifle and a pistol, Budd prepared to defend himself against six bandits. Only the bandits never returned.

Budd waited and waited.

He leaned against the rocks until the sun began to set, mouth dried out from the windless air. Heat still radiated off the stones. They brushed against his reddened skin as he finally stood up and left his cover. A coyote signaled the coming of nightfall. Bats screeched as they fluttered across the blue-streaked sky.

Budd looked toward the canyons. Black smoke appeared in the distance. He followed the dark stream of smoke until his feet throbbed. Flat, sandy earth gave way to rocky terrain. The golden light of a campfire illuminated the valley below the canyon. Budd crouched low and kept his back against the rock wall. He looked around the corner and saw a merchant cart filled with ammunition, gun crates, and explosives.

It must have been the wagon that was stolen from Mr. Maguire. The wagon that had been reported back when Pratt Dempcy first expanded their business to California. Budd looked beyond the wagon and over to a cave nearby. The same six masked men who attacked the stagecoach sat around a blazing fire. They poked at a cast-iron pot that dangled above the crackling embers as they argued with each other.

"We need to find him before he makes it to town," said the bandit, who sat near the mouth of the cave. "Last thing we need is a bunch of lawmen breathing down our necks."

"Let's just let him die out in the desert. Won't make it more than a day or two without water. Not in this heat," said another bandit.

Budd licked his chapped lips as he watched them pass around a water canteen. He gripped his rifle tight. His eyes scanned for any sign of a vantage point. Only steep rock walls surrounded them, and there was no way his feet would carry him back toward the entrance of the valley. Budd knew he had no choice but to fight.

He reached into his satchel and pulled out a matchbox. The wagon provided the cover of darkness as he rustled around for a stick of dynamite and rifle ammo. Budd struck the match, lit the fuse, tossed the dynamite into the wagon, and ran as fast as he could away from the cave.

Chapter 13

Black Lake, California

They had drawn a heart with a crown of thorns upon the wall of the bank manager's office. Someone had haphazardly scribbled the mark of the Royal Hearts gang in black ink. Dotty traced the symbol of her family's legacy with the tip of her finger. The symbol was wrong, tainted somehow. She smiled as she counted the thorns. "Nine instead of seven… curious."

"What is curious?" Sheriff Dawson asked.

"There are nine thorns. The Royal Hearts use seven thorns on the crown to represent my father and his comrades," Dotty explained. "I believe a member of the Blood Eagles drew this."

Sheriff Baker and Sheriff Dawson exchanged looks. Their skepticism had been expected. Dotty knew no lawman had ever trusted her family. And she was certain many of her father's rival gangs had bought a number of sheriffs in the region.

Dotty continued, "Only a former member of the Royal Hearts would make the mistake of drawing nine thorns. It is an outdated version of my father's symbol."

Sheriff Baker walked Dotty and Dawson out of the Bank Manager's office and back out into the lobby. Dotty counted the bullet casings and concluded the outlaw had robbed the bank without a plan. She followed the casings over to a discarded Colt single-action revolver that looked relatively new despite the burn mark from a bullet.

"You shot the gun out of his hand?" Dotty asked Sheriff Baker.

"Yes, ma'am."

"During the shootout, you never once attempted to shoot the robber? Only disarm him?" she questioned. "Seems unusual for both a lawman of your skill and an outlaw capable of robbing a bank alone to walk away from a gunfight unscathed. Don't you think?"

"What exactly are you implying?" Sheriff Baker straightened to his full height, as if he wanted to intimidate Dotty. "I did what I could."

Sheriff Dawson pulled Dotty aside before she gave Baker a piece of her mind. "Careful where you go tossing around accusations," he warned. "Folks in California ain't too trusting. Especially toward anyone with the name Valentine."

Dotty crossed her arms and stood her ground. "This robbery feels all wrong, Sheriff. I can feel it in my bones, and he knows something about it."

"Are you sure this isn't your gang's work?" Dawson asked. "They could have drawn it in a hurry."

"If Budd was here..." Dotty bit her lip and blinked away the unshed tears of frustration in her eyes. "That stagecoach should have been back to Sacramento by now. Budd is missing and—"

"Hold it right there," Sheriff Dawson said. "Budd Mansfield isn't missing. He's been gone for less than a day. The stagecoach could have been delayed."

"Have you ever known him to go off schedule? Because he doesn't seem the sort to me." Dotty tapped her foot nervously. She hadn't known Budd Mansfield long, but he was a man of lasting impressions. "Budd might be out in that desert right now, and we're wasting time with this robbery. I'm telling you, something isn't right about all this."

Dotty left Sheriff Dawson where he stood and surveyed the area once more. There were pristine shell casings, and some that had clearly been made at a campfire or stove. She picked up one that had been carved with the mark of the Blood Eagles. Dotty smiled victoriously and tossed it at Sheriff Baker.

The lawman caught the spent shell just before it hit the floor. "What's this?"

"Proof," Dotty began. "The ace of spades is proof this was not my father's gang but the work of a desperate band of outlaws still clinging to the past."

Baker held up the shell casing as Dawson moved closer. The lawmen inspected the mark closely. Dawson looked as if the shell casing had chipped away at some of the distrust he harbored for Dotty. But Dotty saw fear in the eyes of Sheriff Baker.

"Th-this don't mean nothin'," said Baker. "He could have found this anywhere and used it in the robbery."

"I think if we find where he dumped more of these, they will lead us down the exact path the robber took. Maybe it'll even lead us to where they stashed the money." Dotty had chosen her words carefully. She watched Sheriff Baker with sharp eyes, tracking each tiny movement he made. The lawman had grown significantly more jittery since her arrival, and Dotty suspected it had little to do with her being a woman.

She followed one pile of dumped casings to another near the columns outside the bank. Dawson copied her steps carefully. Dotty led him across the road and over to the general store, where the shopkeeper had been killed in the crossfire. "Nearly a dozen men had been shooting. Three deputies were injured, and they gunned a shopkeeper down, but they hurt no one else. The sheriff got into a tussle with the robber, but we spared him."

Dawson nodded along. "I understand your suspicion. My thoughts were similar, but if we're going to sort this out, we need to be careful with what we say around those we suspect."

Dotty kneeled down and brushed away some flour. She picked up a scrap of paper and unfolded it. "Telegram from Ripley Eagleson," Dotty sighed. "Telling Salazar to lie low in Black Lake. Must have fallen from his pocket."

"So… Ripley Eagleson really is the leader of the Blood Eagles." There was awe in Sheriff Dawson's voice.

"You never knew?" Dotty asked.

"Evan Farris suspected he was connected somehow, but we never confirmed it." Sheriff Dawson looked down at his boots and sighed. "I should have listened to him when I had the chance. But I know someone who had a run-in with Eagleson—someone who might tell us a thing or two about the gang. Name is Reginald Pearce, and his brother-in-law, John Pepper, was part of the Blood Eagles."

"Can we speak with John?"

Dawson finally met Dotty's gaze. He rocked back and forth on his heels and said, "Budd Mansfield killed John Pepper. There was a shootout at a cabin up in Yosemite Valley. John and Budd struggled over a gun. Budd barely made it out alive."

Dotty glanced back down at the telegram. "I'm sorry, Sheriff, but if the Blood Eagles are declaring war, I have to tell my father. Ripley Eagleson is a monster. He'll smile in your face while he holds a gun to your head." She then looked from the telegram to Sheriff Baker near the entrance of the bank. "And he has purchased the dignity and pride of too many lawmen for my comfort."

"Is that your way of telling me you're going after Mansfield?"

"I will give him until morning," Dotty stated firmly. "If he isn't in Sacramento by sunrise, I'll take a posse and search Calligan Road."

***

Somewhere in the desert

The wagon erupted into a ball of fire. Bullets broke through the ammunition crates and ricocheted off the canyon walls. Budd dropped down and covered his head with his arms, praying to God he might live to see another day. Fiery debris fell from the sky. Sparks snapped, casting flashes of light that broke through the shadows.

Voices called out from inside the cave. "Find who did that and bring me their heads!"

A cloud of dust wrapped around Budd.

He slithered across the ground as he moved further away from the bandits. The rifle in his hand felt heavier by the second. Budd sat up against the rock wall and took aim. He stared down the sights at the red-haired bandit with a pistol. The outlaw fired in Budd's direction. Budd kept both eyes open as he pulled the trigger and dropped the man with a bullet to the knee. The other bandits turned to him.

His only cover came in the wagon's form, which still blazed in the night. Sparks grazed his shoulder, but he felt none of it. Budd fired a second time and missed his mark. The pounding in his head silenced the endless cacophony of gunfire. He flipped the lever on his rifle and ejected the shell, reloaded the chamber, cocked the hammer, and fired again and again. Each time he squeezed the trigger, the bandits changed position.

It disoriented Budd as their black clothes moved against the dark sky. It caused his aim to falter. Quick, stealthy movements marked them as professionals, not just ordinary outlaws. His only hope of survival was distraction. And nothing distracted an outlaw more than a blow to their ego. "You call yourselves a gang?" he shouted above the sounds of battle. "I've fought men worth more than all six of you combined."

A bandit exited the cave. "Hold fire."

Budd looked up at the man who had issued the order. Even with the dark mask and the shadows, Budd felt a surge of recognition. Had the outlaw from the wanted posters been the leader of the Blood Eagles all along? Budd wondered. Salazar Torez had a thick accent, however, and the man who attacked the stagecoaches had more of a twang.

"Where's your boss?" Budd asked.

"Do you see anyone else in charge here, gringo?"

"I'll make myself clear," he replied as he stepped out from behind cover. "Where is Ripley Eagleson, and why did he send you after the stagecoach?"

"I don't know anyone by that name."

Budd reached for his hat before he remembered it had been thrown from the stagecoach. He ran his fingers through his hair and winced when he felt a large lump. "Hard to believe, seeing as he and I entered an arrangement not too long ago. And if I recall correctly... you were there too. Yes, I'd know those eyes anywhere."

"You might be a little loco," Salazar chuckled. "I think you hit your head too hard when you fell from the stagecoach." More laughter echoed in the cave.

Budd backed away slowly, keeping his eyes on the men as they surrounded their leader. He pulled back on the hammer of his rifle. "Perhaps I am a little crazy. But I wager I can still beat you in a duel."

Salazar's eyes narrowed. "What are the terms?"

"Quick draw to disarm only," Budd said. "You win and I surrender without a fight. I'm guessing I'd make a pretty nice bargaining chip between you and your boss. And if I win, I take one of them horses, and I leave here alive."

Budd counted the seconds as he waited for Salazar's answer. He knew his value among outlaws. He also knew

Salazar had been on the bank robbery posters back in Black Lake. Budd wasn't afraid to gamble if his opponent had nothing to lose as well.

"What do you say?" he urged. "We got a deal?"

Salazar nodded. The outlaw gestured to his men as he removed the mask from his face. Budd watched closely as Salazar walked ten paces to the right and held his hand over the revolver at his hip. The others pulled their injured man into the cave and stayed out of sight. But Budd felt their eyes glaring at his face as he slung his rifle over his back.

He took up a position across from Salazar. Only the pale light of the moon and the burning wagon lit up the hollow valley of the canyon. Budd squinted until he saw every detail of Salazar's face. He gave the signal and lowered his hand to his side. Five. Four. Three. Bang!

A bullet tore through the flesh of his thigh before he finished the countdown. Budd fell to his knees. He breathed heavily through his nose and swallowed back the bile that burned the back of his throat. Budd's vision went red with untamed fury. He unholstered his gun and fired off three shots.

Three shots fired. Three outlaws cried out in pain. They ran for the cave. Budd rolled behind the wagon.

Salazar opened fire. "You thought I would let you win?" he scoffed. "I have heard the legends, gringo. I know what they say about you."

Budd removed his jacket and tore the sleeve off his shirt. He wrapped the scrap of fabric around his thigh to stop the bleeding. His fingers trembled as he cocked the hammer on his revolver. Budd took a deep breath and said, "I should thank you."

"What for?"

Budd stood up on shaky legs and watched Salazar for any sign of weakness. Salazar's holster was on the right, but he held his gun with the left hand. And Budd remembered when Dotty had told him she had shot one bandit in the shoulder.

It explained why Salazar used his left hand in the duel. "For letting me know I don't have to play by the rules," Budd answered.

Chapter 14

Sacramento, California

Dotty slammed her hands onto Sheriff Dawson's desk. She stared him down with every bit of anger she felt burning in her hazel eyes. They had been arguing for hours. Dawn had come and gone, and still he refused to search for Budd.

"Then let me form a posse of my own, and I'll search every inch of the desert," she pleaded. "He would do it for you."

Sheriff Dawson looked unfazed by her brazen display. "We have people missing, Miss Valentine. I can't just put their search on hold for Budd Mansfield. We need to recover the stagecoach that went missing, and I need every available person to do so. I simply can't spare anyone for your posse."

The door opened suddenly.

Blake and Steven Wright tossed an ace of spades onto Sheriff Dawson's desk. Blake moved in front of his brother and tapped his finger on the playing card. "It was a setup," he claimed. "We were out all night looking for Mansfield. All we found was a dead body, and an abandoned stagecoach."

"A body?" Sheriff Dawson stood up and finally turned his attention to the issue. "Was it Mansfield or the driver?"

"That's the thing," Steven Wright said. "The driver, the shotgun man, and the other two passengers were nowhere to be found. There are horse tracks around where we found the stagecoach. Looks like they abandoned the man and left him to die in the wild."

Dotty picked up the card and scrutinized it. "They wanted Mansfield."

"That's what we think," replied Blake. He and his brother looked from Sheriff Dawson to Dotty. "Are you puttin' together a search?"

Dawson threw his hands up in the air and shouted, "Hold on! We don't know what happened. And until I have proof the driver and the guard were behind the attack, I want my people out there looking for them and the other passengers."

"You're wasting time." Dotty sniffled. She wiped her eyes before the tears fell, but she still felt a lump in her throat. "If Budd is still alive, he doesn't have long before the heat gets him. Do what you want... I'm going on my own. It's what Budd would do."

"We're going with you." Blake Wright patted his brother on the back, and the two of them followed Dotty out to the horses.

Ivory, Budd Mansfield's mare gave her an odd look when she reached for the reins. The temperamental horse fussed as Dotty climbed into the saddle. It took a while before the mount settled. She ran her fingers through the horse's mane, trying her best to soothe the old girl's nerves.

When Ivory finally eased up, Dotty steered her toward the main road that cut through the city. "We'll start at Calligan Road and go all the way to Black Lake or Timber if we have to," she told the Wright Brothers.

"Evan Farris would have wanted us to do this. We're with you until the end, Dotty," said Steven Wright. "Besides, if we're right about this, it'll be a pleasure to watch Sheriff Dawson's face turn red again."

Blake snorted at his brother's retort.

Dotty allowed herself to smile, even though it felt hollow. She kept her eyes trained straight ahead, focusing on the task at hand. The witty banter between the brothers faded into the background as Dotty led them to the edge of the city.

Small farms and family homes lined the many dirt roads that peppered the land. Only a few trees were scattered about the dry waves of amber grass.

It was about noon when Dotty and the Wright brothers finally reached Calligan Road. They passed by the folks who searched for the missing passengers and the deputies accompanying them. Still, Dotty kept her eyes from wandering.

She scoured the long dirt road, but it had been impossible to tell which tracks might have been Budd's. Far too many people had trampled over the trail for her to be certain.

When they happened upon the abandoned stagecoach, Dotty spotted two sets of tracks. "Some lead to Sacramento, and the others lead to the desert," she said aloud. "The driver or gunman wouldn't have gone further into danger."

"Then these must be from the bandits," Blake said.

"Wait," Steven interjected. He dropped down from his horse and circled around the wagon. "There's a third set of tracks here. Heading northeast toward the Yosemite Valley trail. At least four horses."

"Budd said he and Evan had a run-in with the Blood Eagles in Yosemite Valley." Dotty pinched the bridge of her nose as she tried to concentrate. "Could the driver and shotgun man have met up with the gang to exchange the loot before they split up?"

Blake nodded. "It's possible. Perhaps they went separate ways in case the law might come lookin' for them."

Steven reached out for Dotty, but dropped his hand before it reached her. "Three trails and an unknown number of bandits? I'm sorry, Dotty, but it ain't lookin' too good for Mansfield."

"I'm not going back until I bring him home or we find a body," she snapped. "I... I still need his help." The lie tasted bitter on her tongue. In fact, Dotty wasn't sure why she cared so much about a man she barely knew. If it had been anyone else, she would have looked the other way.

But Budd Mansfield was different. He looked at Dotty as if he saw more than an outlaw's daughter. And that alone made him worth saving in her eyes. Dotty needed at least one person left in the world who saw beyond her facade.

"We have to split up," she said as she dug around in Budd's saddle bag. Dotty pulled out a flare gun. "Do all of you carry one of these?"

"Budd made every guard get one in case of situations like this," Blake answered.

"You take the right, Blake. Steven, you take the Yosemite trail. I'll head deeper into the desert. If we find him or we need help, shoot the flare up into the sky," Dotty ordered. "We regroup here at nightfall."

"Yes, ma'am."

"You got it, boss."

Dotty guided Ivory toward the canyons in the distance. It would have been the best cover from the sun or the best way to avoid an ambush. Even in her thinnest skirt and blouse, Dotty felt the afternoon heat seep into her skin. Sweat beaded on her upper lip and the small of her back.

Budd must have suffered out in the open, with nowhere to go but further away from civilization.

She tried to imagine how he might have wandered aimlessly in search of anything more than rock and sand. Just the thought of such misery made her heart clench. Dotty reached for the water canteen strapped to the saddle bag. She uncapped the lid and brought it to her lips. Warm water rushed into her mouth and spilled down her neck.

Dotty nearly dropped the canteen as gunshots reverberated from the canyon. She lifted the flare gun and fired toward the sun. Red smoke trailed from the end of the gun before it blew away in the wind. Two more flares went up, and Dotty urged Ivory into a gallop.

***

Somewhere in the desert

Budd ran as fast as his injured leg allowed. He made his way over to a deep crack in the canyon wall and slid in as far as he could. Only two rounds remained in the small box of rifle ammo he grabbed from the wagon before he set it ablaze.

Budd reloaded his rifle and checked the number of rounds in his pistol. Three remained in the cylinder, along with a handful in his pocket.

Things looked grim for Budd Mansfield.

Though the bandits had four injured men, they had nearly a dozen guns between them, as well as an unknown number of bullets. Budd wasn't sure how long he could hold them off before surrendering, but he wasn't ready to give up just yet.

There was unfinished business that he needed to tend to before he left this earth. So Budd shut his eyes and prayed to God he had just a little more fight left in him.

"Come on out, gringo!"

Budd fired around the corner and ducked back inside the crevasse in the canyon wall. He licked the sweat from his lips as a hawk soared overhead.

A loud caw echoed through the canyon, breaking through the barrage of gunfire. Budd snuck a peek at Salazar Torez.

The outlaw spoke in a hushed tone and gestured wildly with his hands before the bandits changed position once again.

There was no clear shot.

"I heard you broke out of prison," Budd said. "Must have had some help."

"Sí. I have many friends. But the same cannot be said for you." Salazar paced back and forth in front of the cave. "You worked for the Pinkertons, yes?"

"Seems like ages ago."

Salazar shook his head. "I do not believe you, señor. The kind of work you and I do leaves a man scarred."

Budd slipped out from behind his cover, leaving himself vulnerable. He limped closer to Salazar as his anger boiled over. "We are not the same! My work helps people."

"So does mine," the outlaw snickered. "I have a family that needs feeding. What I do, I do for them."

It wasn't the same, and he reckoned Salazar knew that. In fact, Budd was convinced Salazar had baited him out of his hiding spot… and he had fallen right into the outlaw's trap.

He shuffled back and tripped. Budd scooted himself with one hand as he raised his rifle. He squeezed the trigger and heard the click of an empty barrel.

Budd tossed the rifle aside. He crawled toward the crevasse, but the pain in his leg was too much. Bullets hit the ground right next to his hands. Hooves pounded in his ears like drums. Someone grabbed him by the arms and dragged him onto the back of a horse.

The bandits shouted profanities. Salazar Torez gave chase on foot, but the horse was too quick. Budd tipped over and hit the ground just before he lost consciousness.

***

"Rise and shine, Mr. Mansfield," a voice called from the shadows of his mind. Budd opened his eyes with a grimace. Blinding light spilled over the canyon walls, scorching everything in the valley below. He blinked past the film over his eyes until a man's face became clearer—a man he recognized instantly as Reginald Pearce.

"There you are," Reginald said. "Thought I lost you for a minute. Gave me quite the fright."

"There are… bandits." Budd sat up and nearly toppled over.

Reginald steadied him with one hand and offered water with the other. The man looked out of place in the desert with his fancy suit and slicked-back hair.

"I know," Reginald said. "They're hunkered down in that cave. I guess you put up quite the fight. It's impressive for a man in your condition."

"How long was I unconscious?"

"Only an hour." Reginald peeled back the fabric wrapped around Budd's thigh. "This looks bad. Might be infected, but I have nothing to patch you up with. It will have to wait until we can get you to town."

"What are you doing out here?" Budd asked finally. "This ain't exactly the place for a man like you. No offense."

"I was riding out to Oakhill Farm when I heard gunshots," Reginald explained. "Bandits on the road were whispering about how you might have survived a fall from a stagecoach. Thought I would come out here and see if you were alive for myself."

Budd's stomach dropped. He braced his hands on the ground and pushed himself up into a sitting position. "Are you here to avenge that brother-in-law of yours? Because Johnny was an evil man. He gave me no choice but to defend myself."

"Would I have dragged you beneath this overhang and kept you alive if I was here to kill you?" Reginald laughed through his nose. "It's a bit much."

Budd shook his head. "I'm grateful, really. I just ain't in the habit of trusting folks." He drank more water and stared over at the cave where the bandits had camped out. "They think I'm dead, don't they?"

Reginald shrugged. "Perhaps. Or they're getting ready for another attack."

"We ain't making it out of this valley if we don't fight," Budd said. "There's about two miles between us and the mouth of the canyon. I'm down a leg, and you can't carry me all the way there." He gripped onto the wall and pulled himself up. Dizziness overwhelmed him. Budd breathed heavily as he tried to steady himself.

"I'd suggest you take my horse and leave, but they might just shoot you in the back on your way out." Reginald sighed. "But maybe I could talk to them."

"No. It's too risky."

"They aren't after me, Mr. Mansfield."

There was a moment where Budd actually considered going through with Reginald's plan. However, there was a part of him that couldn't take the risk—even with someone he suspected was more than what he appeared. There had been a time when he thought Reginald Pearce and Ripley Eagleson were one and the same.

Suspicion still lingered, but Budd now owed Reginald his life. And his unexpected savior deserved a chance to make it out of the canyon alive and well.

Chapter 15

Ripley Eagleson had mastered the art of deception many years before he became Reginald Pearce. Of course, it had been difficult for him as he built such a sterling reputation. But there were moments when the benefits had been worth the trouble. Moments like when he saved Budd Mansfield's life and the untrusting brute didn't suspect him of treachery.

"Let me talk to their leader," he suggested once more. "Perhaps we can come to an understanding." Rip walked over to his horse and opened a bag tied to the saddle. He showed stacks of cash to Budd Mansfield—a man who seemed entirely unfazed by the sight of such a tempting amount of money.

"You want to bribe a bandit?" Mansfield looked over the rocks that provided them cover and stared at the cave. "He'll rob you and then he'll shoot you."

"It's a risk I'm willing to take if it buys you enough time to ride out of here."

"Why would you do that?" Mansfield asked. "I ain't done nothing to earn your trust, much less an act of selflessness like that."

"My brother-in-law was part of their gang," Rip reminded him. "I've had my fair share of run-ins with outlaws. He can take the money and leave if he lets us out of the blasted desert alive. This man is toying with you, Mr. Mansfield. He has men, he has horses, and he has guns. He could have killed you by now, but he didn't."

Mansfield nodded. "I was thinking the same thing. He's buying time for something… or someone."

"Either way, this may be our only chance." Rip unhooked the bag of money and slung it over his shoulder. "I was going to use this money to buy Oakhill Farm for my sister. It will be better spent saving our lives."

"You're a lucky man," Mansfield supposed. "Having something to live for makes all the difference in the world. I never knew my family."

Rip helped Mansfield up and held him steady until he could balance on his own. Circumstances had made Mansfield Rip's enemy. If the security manager hadn't gotten in the way of the stagecoach robberies, they might have been allies. But the man's stubborn pursuit of justice had placed them firmly on opposite sides of the law. There was simply too much blood spilled between them.

In another life, perhaps Reginald and Budd could have been friends, but Ripley Eagleson was no one's friend. He was a predator that swam in a sea of prey. "Maybe this was a sign from God," he said. "A sign that it's time you find something worth living for."

"You might be right, but that don't mean I can just ride away without knowing—"

"I'm not giving you a choice." Rip whistled for his horse and held the reins as he gave Mansfield a pointed look. The insufferable man finally gave in and hoisted himself into the saddle with a hiss.

"I'll send a search party for you. I promise," Mansfield said.

Rip nodded. He raised his arms and walked away from the horse, slowly making his way toward Salazar Torez. What the security manager didn't know was there was a sly grin on Ripley Eagleson's face. Salazar saw his approach and exited the cave. The two of them stared each other down.

"You're late," Salazar said. "And you helped him."

"Plans have changed." Rip's eyes squinted against the sunlight. "I had to kill a telegram operator to stop him from sending the sheriff's message to the U.S. Marshal's office. Seems your mistake caught the law's attention."

"What mistake?"

Rip slapped Sal across the face so hard that his hand throbbed. It happened so quickly, it had been barely visible to the naked eye. "You were supposed to steal the money and kill Mansfield in the struggle."

"We thought he was dead before he blew up the weapons," Sal explained. "If the fall hadn't killed him, the desert should have."

"He is very much alive." Rip dropped the money at Sal's feet. "Take it and go. I have to stay behind and try to fix this mess. Tell me when he's out of sight."

Sal leaned to the side, eyes pinned to Budd Mansfield's back until he disappeared around the bend. When Sal gave the signal, Rip lowered his arms. He walked past Sal and entered the cave where some of the weapon crates were stashed, along with several crates of explosives. Rip muttered under his breath. It wasn't enough to take on a small town like Black Lake, let alone a city like Sacramento.

"There was supposed to be one last job," he said to no one in particular. "We were supposed to hit Pratt Dempcy's office for the insurance money and fight our way out of the city. But now we have to smuggle more guns! Fools! All of you!"

The hired guns ignored Rip as Sal handed over several handfuls of cash to each man who had been brought on for the robbery. Once they were paid, the hired guns rode out of the valley with their cut—leaving Salazar and Rip alone in the cave.

"Hit me," Rip ordered Salazar. "Beat me a little and fire a few rounds into the air. I can't go back to town untouched."

The first punch came as a surprise. The second, third, and even fourth punches landed with a fury that made Rip suspicious of Salazar. He wondered how long the outlaw had been waiting for the day he could fight back.

But it was the kick to the gut that threw Rip over the edge. He hit the ground and swept his leg under Sal's feet, knocking the outlaw onto his back. Rip rolled on top of Sal and pounded his fist into his face.

Sal bucked Rip off and ran for his horse.

"Get back to the Old Mill and send the others to gather the guns," Rip slurred through swollen lips. He flexed his aching jaw and spit a mouthful of blood into the dirt. His ears rang from the force of Sal's punches.

Rip used the wall of the cave to pull himself up as three shots rang through the canyon.

"And then you wait for orders. Do you understand, Salazar?"

"Yes, boss."

***

Goldcap Canyon, California

Ivory tossed her mane and galloped toward a lone horse in the canyon valley. Dotty let the horse lead. She kept her eyes on their target with her hand hovering over her revolver. It wasn't until a cloud passed over the sun that she saw who the rider was.

Budd Mansfield. He flashed a lopsided grin and chuckled, "You came for me."

"Of course I did," Dotty said. "When the stagecoach never returned… I just knew something was wrong. Everyone told me I was being paranoid, but I felt in my heart that you were in trouble."

Budd rode up beside Ivory. "Thank you, Dotty. If yours is the last face I see before I die, then I'll have died a fortunate man. You've proven yourself to be a good friend." His eyes rolled into the back of his skull, and Budd Mansfield slumped forward in the saddle.

Fear and confusion stole Dotty's breath away. "Budd! Hold on!" she called. Dotty pulled back on the reins and slowed Ivory's pace. She hopped down from the saddle and ran over to him.

He was barely conscious, draped over the back of a pedigree horse, and clutching his leg with pale fingers. "I got you," she whispered as she reached up for him.

He blinked weakly as he slid off the saddle.

Dotty broke Budd's fall with her own body as he fell off the horse. She rolled out from under the large man and looked at his wound.

Infection had already set in. "I'm here," Dotty said as tears stung her eyes. "The others are on their way. I signaled for help as soon as I heard shots."

Budd reached down and snagged Dotty's hand. "Thank you... Even if I don't make it, I just want to say thank you."

She shook her head. Tears spilled from her eyes. "That sounds like a goodbye, Budd Mansfield. And I'm not giving up on you. Stay with me. Keep breathing. That's it."

Dotty pulled the bullet free and tossed it in the sand. She pressed her hand to the wound and prayed quietly. Dark spots appeared on his dusty shirt as her tears dotted the fabric.

Blake and Steven arrived with a small wagon hitched to their horses. "We found this near the road. We thought you might want to—" Blake's words cut off at the sight of Budd. He waved his brother along and hurried over to help Dotty.

The Wright boys lifted Budd onto the back of the small wagon. Dotty climbed in after they settled Budd. She used the knife from her boot and cut away the stained cloth surrounding the bullet wound.

Her heart stopped for a moment. Dotty took the water canteen from his hand and poured some over his leg. Then, Dorothy Valentine tried her best to save a man she barely knew.

A man she had quickly admired for his selflessness and morals.

"Reginald..."

"Who?" Dotty asked. She leaned over Budd and got close enough to hear his words. "Who is Reginald, Budd? Come on. Talk to me."

Bright blue eyes reflected a cerulean sky. "He saved me. We have to help him."

"If he saved you, then we will," she replied. "Rest now."

Everything else drifted away. In her mind, there were just the two of them and that tiny wagon. She placed herself in a position that kept him from getting jostled too much, legs braced against the sides as they rode out of the desert.

Her eyes flickered from his leg to his face, searching for signs of consciousness or bleeding. Budd faded in and out. But Dotty noticed how hard he fought to stay awake.

"Blake," she said. "Can you go back to the canyon and see if you can find a man named Reginald? He saved Budd's life."

"Sure thing," Blake answered. "I'll try to get back here as soon as I can."

Once Blake rode away, Steven snapped the reins and moved the wagon on.

Dotty tore off the end of her skirt and bandaged Budd's leg. She then tilted his head back and poured water into his mouth.

His eyes fluttered as he drank. When Budd was finished, Dotty carefully laid him back down. She watched him closely until he finally succumbed to exhaustion.

His chest rose and fell slowly as Dotty counted the seconds between breaths. Seconds that quickly turned into minutes.

"Go faster!" Dotty shouted to Steven. "We're losing him!"

The wagon lurched forward. Rattling deafened Dotty to all other sounds as they barreled toward Calligan Road. Clouds of dust and dirt flew by, stinging her eyes.

She threw herself over Budd and shielded him with her body. Every bump in the road tossed them up into the air, causing them to bounce off the floor of the wagon.

"We won't make it back to the city in time," Steven shouted above the noise.

"Then take us to Oakhill Farm." Dotty held Budd in her arms until the wagon slowed. She panted heavily, dragging ragged breaths into her lungs.

When she finally had the courage to open her eyes, her gaze landed on Budd's chest. The rise and fall had stopped somewhere along the way. Dotty pressed her ear to his chest. He was alive, but barely.

Dotty's fear had been so intense that she hadn't noticed when Steven fetched the farmer and one worker. They dragged Budd from her hands and carried him inside the quaint little farmhouse.

Dotty had no choice but to follow quietly, still shocked by the thought of losing Budd Mansfield. He had been rude to her and dismissive of her problems, but beneath it all, she saw him for what he was.

Budd Mansfield was a good man—a better man than the world deserved. And she was determined to save his life.

So Dotty stayed by his side and helped any way she could. The farmer rode into town and fetched the doctor. After hours of their collective efforts, Budd Mansfield's eyes fluttered open once more.

He met her gaze with so much warmth that Dotty felt as if her heart had skipped a beat.

Chapter 16

Oakhill Farm

Black Lake, California

The cloying smell of sickness wrapped around him. Something foul burned at the back of his throat. Budd Mansfield peeled open his eyelids and rolled onto his side before he expelled the contents of his stomach onto the floor.

Someone rushed in and helped him, rinsed his mouth with water, and put him back onto the bed. He squinted, tried to see who his fallen angel had been, but the fog had quickly closed in around him again.

Familiar voices faded in and out.

There was a moment when Budd even thought he heard Evan calling out to him from somewhere in the darkness. Part of him thought he was dead. The other half prayed he was.

Pain came in waves, crashing over him like the tide. Fevers caused him to shiver, even when his sweat soaked through the linens. And yet Budd reckoned it could have been worse for him if not for the angel in his room.

"Wake up, ugly," said Blake Wright.

Budd blinked rapidly and glanced over at the surly hired gun and his brother. Beside them was Evan Farris. His friend looked good—healthy, even.

There was color to Evan's cheeks and a smile upon his face, which was more than what Budd could ever have hoped for. "H-how long...?"

"How long have you been unconscious?" Evan finished. "Five days. Would have been longer if not for Dotty taking such good care of you."

Budd turned his head to the other side of the room, where Dorothy Valentine sat. She gave him a look he couldn't decipher and went back to sewing up a hole in one of his shirts.

Budd wasn't sure why he felt such a surge of joy at the sight of her, but he was grateful for all she had done. Few strangers would have nursed him back to health. But... Dotty wasn't just a stranger anymore, he reckoned.

Evan cleared his throat and drew Budd's attention away from Dotty.

Budd had ignored the smirk on his friend's face and asked, "What happened to Reginald?"

"He was beaten, but I found him alive," said Blake. "He sent them runnin' after they took the money from him. Got to say I wasn't expectin' such a fight from a suit-wearin' city boy like him."

Budd nodded.

Reginald Pearce had surprised him as well. The first time Budd met the man had been when John Pepper murdered a stagecoach driver in cold blood. But while it had convinced Evan Reginald was Ripley Eagleson, Budd had trouble associating the two after the man saved his life.

Would a hardened criminal have risked his life to save Budd? The lines between friend and enemy were more blurred than ever.

"I need to get back to Sacramento. Sheriff Dawson should know what he's up against," Budd said finally.

He scooted himself up against the headboard. It was clear he hadn't been in the infirmary. The room was decorated with lace and quilted blankets, far homier than any physician's office Budd had been to.

But the expressions on Evan's, Blake's, and Steven's faces were anything but welcoming.

Steven was the one who spoke up. "Sheriff Dawson and his deputies just finished scouring the region. The passengers you rode with are missin' and so are the driver and the shotgun man."

"I don't understand."

Blake moved to the side of the bed and said, "It was a setup. We all think you and a writer for the newspaper were the only real passengers."

"What about the bandits? Were they captured?"

"We were hoping you could convince Reginald Pearce to identify them," Evan replied. "We looked in that cave, and there was nothing but spent shells and empty crates. Someone went back and cleaned it out."

Budd wanted to scream in frustration. "They were going to kill me, weren't they? Just take me out and make it look like I died defending the coach."

"But they failed," Dotty stated. She set the shirt aside and stood up from her chair. The heels of her shoes clicked on the hardwood floor as she drew closer to the bed.

"They didn't kill you, so now we need to understand why they needed you out of the way."

"I got close to finding out about the stolen guns, and they got scared. Or they figured they were running out of time before the mayor and Sheriff Dawson sent for a marshal."

Budd scratched at his stubbled jaw and yawned. Though he had slept for five days, he still felt tired from all the fighting in the canyon. Hours upon hours of firing into the darkness had drained all his energy.

Dotty seemed to sense his exhaustion, for she eased him back down to the pillows. Evan, Brett, and Steven left the room without further discussion—most likely out of fear that Dotty's legendary temper would erupt.

Once alone, Dotty pulled the chair close to Budd's bedside and placed her hand in his. "You frightened me," she said. "I thought we lost you a few times. And I realize now that I would be very hurt if ever—"

"I'm all right," he interjected. Budd squeezed her hand reassuringly. "I'm alive and breathing, thanks to you and Reginald Pearce."

"Would you like to see him?" Dotty offered. "I can arrange for him to visit you here after supper."

Budd asked, "Where exactly is here? I remember little after getting in the wagon, and even that ain't too clear."

Dotty dropped Budd's hand and smoothed down his blanket. "Oakhill Farm. Mr. Daniels and his sons were kind enough to take us in while you heal."

Budd added the kind man and his family to the list of people he owed. It wasn't like him to be indebted to others. It made him feel weak and helpless.

The way Dotty fussed over him was just another blow to his dignity. But Budd wasn't sure he had the heart to tell her to stop. Instead, he suffered in silence.

"I'll wake you when Reginald arrives," she whispered. "I'm sure the two of you have a lot to discuss. But it'll be a long time before you're able to get out of bed, I'm afraid."

The gentle tone of her voice chased away his doubts and filled him with warmth. Warmth that seeped into his achy bones and pulled him to sleep.

Budd allowed himself to drift away as he sank into the mattress beneath him.

***

Sacramento, California
Four days later

Ripley Eagleson had never imagined a day where he would ride side by side with Budd Mansfield. But, alas, that day had come. And Rip trembled with the urge to shoot the man right there and then. He squeezed his hands into fists and bit down on the inside of his cheek. The worthless fool prattled on and on about justice and good deeds.

"So you are on a mission to right some wrongs," Rip said. "I can understand that."

Budd Mansfield's hand dropped to where he had been shot. There was still a telltale bulge from a bandage that strained against his pant leg. "I've made mistakes. There's no doubt about that. I see no harm in trying to make amends."

Rip led Budd to the saloon and hitched his horse to the post outside. Storm flicked his ears and drank from the trough. Budd hitched his mare beside Storm.

When the horses were settled, they wandered into the saloon. The doors swung closed behind them with a squeak. Rip spotted the group of hired guns that Sal paid in the back corner. He made a subtle gesture in their direction, and Budd Mansfield's gaze hardened.

"Have a seat and order a drink," Budd ordered. "I'll go make the arrest." He pulled a deputy's badge from his pocket and pinned it over his heart.

Rip watched quietly as Budd approached the mercenaries. He was too far away to hear the conversation, but it was not long before one aimed a gun right at Budd's chest. Budd flipped his gun from the holster and shot the gun out of the man's hand.

Four mercenaries lunged for Budd while the fifth ran for the door. Rip looked on intensely as Mansfield fought with a fury few men possessed. The largest mercenary threw Budd on top of the table, and it broke beneath his weight.

Deputy Evan Farris caught the runner at the back door and tossed him over the bar. Blake and Steven Wright blocked the exits.

Sheriff Dawson tipped his hat at Rip and muttered, "Morning, Reginald."

"Good morning, Sheriff." Rip jutted his chin toward the mercenaries. "It was those five right there. I saw them with my own eyes."

"It's brave of you to come along and help. Most witnesses are too afraid."

"I'm happy to help when I can." Rip shook hands with the lawman and exited the saloon. He grabbed Storm's reins and led the enormous horse over to the stables. He paid the stable master fifty dollars for his discretion before he led Rip to a secret room at the back. An iron door opened, and Hector allowed Rip inside.

"The money is safe at the Old Mill," Salazar announced. "But the city is crawling with badges, and I am not comfortable staying here any longer than we must."

"Yes, I am aware," Rip replied. He removed his jacket and took a seat beside Charles—who had been silent since Rip's arrival.

Rip turned and looked at the nervous outlaw with cruelty glimmering in his eyes. "Your brothers are helping Budd Mansfield. Any way we can change their minds about joining us?"

Charles shook his head. "Last time I spoke with Blake and Steven, they threatened to put a bullet in my belly. They won't see reason."

"Then we have to reach out to what's left of our allies," Rip said. "The sheriff arrested the mercenaries, but it won't be long before they realize it was all a ploy to get them off our trail.

"Ride to Nevada and the Arizona territory. I should still have some contacts there."

Epilogue

Oakhill Farm
Black Lake, California
August 1880

Budd felt a shift in the air, an energy that didn't belong. Someone was in his room. He kept his eyes shut and slipped his hand beneath the pillow in search of his gun. But cold, calloused fingers wrapped around his wrist and squeezed. Budd opened his eyes just as the muzzle of a gun tapped his forehead.

He knocked the gun aside and brought his knee up before he rammed it into his attacker's side. Budd threw himself over the side of the bed and landed on top of the mysterious man. A punch to his ribs forced a pained grunt from his mouth.

But Budd quickly recovered. He bashed the man's gun hand against the floor until the firearm clattered to the ground.

"Mr. Mansfield," said a deep, raspy voice. "I believe you and I have a common enemy."

A lamp flickered to life in the room's corner. Power had been the first word that popped into Budd's mind at the sight of Theodore Valentine. The man was smaller than he had imagined, but he wore an aura of strength like a shield, and Budd respected that.

"Please release my guard," Mr. Valentine chuckled. "Daniel would be very difficult to replace if you killed him."

Budd snatched the gun up and tucked it into the waistband of his trousers. He sat on the edge of the bed and tried to catch his breath.

"What are you doing in Sacramento? Last I heard, you were wanted in this territory."

"Someone tried to blame my gang—my family—for a bank robbery they did not commit," Mr. Valentine replied.

"Now, I cannot sit by and allow that sort of disrespect to go unpunished. Ripley Eagleson—or whoever is leading the Blood Eagles—will answer for it."

"I'm not in the middle of this war," Budd replied.

Mr. Valentine waved a hand at his companion, and the man known only as Daniel handed a letter to Budd. Dotty had written the letter.

Budd was surprised by how detailed she had been in describing the stagecoach robberies and their run-in with the bandits. However, it did not escape his notice just how much she left out regarding her own involvement.

There was no mention of how Dotty had saved his life or defended a stagecoach against six outlaws.

"You put yourself in the middle of it when you recruited my daughter to your cause."

"With all due respect, Mr. Valentine, no one can make your daughter do anything she doesn't want to do." Budd rustled around for a cigarette on the bedside table. He pushed the end between his lips and lit it with a match.

The scent of sulfur and tobacco filled his nostrils as he inhaled the smoke. "She helps me because she knows I'm fighting for peace and justice.,"

"Justice is a matter of perspective," Mr. Valentine said. "It is not something dictated by the law. A bandit might feel as if robbing a stagecoach is an act of justice."

"If you know something I don't, perhaps you should stop talking in riddles and enlighten me." Budd leaned back against the wall and flicked his ashes into a small oak box on the bedside table. There was a moment of great tension that made him uneasy.

It was a silence filled with dark promises. Theodore Valentine was not a man who wasted his time with trivial matters.

"You should speak with your employer about Ripley Eagleson," said Valentine. "They may shed some light on the gang's motives for the robberies.

Haven't you thought it was unusual that the bandits only targeted Pratt Dempcy coaches?"

Budd nodded his head slowly and took a long drag on his cigarette. He wasn't sure what exactly Mr. Valentine had alluded to, but he rolled a few possibilities around in his mind. And none of them had eased the knot in his stomach. The last thing Budd wanted was to find out he worked for a crooked company.

"I'll look into a few possibilities," he said finally. "But that doesn't explain why you're here yourself instead of sending one of your men."

Mr. Valentine stood up. He wore a blood red suit with a black shirt and vest beneath it. Black shoes and silver cufflinks and watch fob completed the bold outfit.

On anyone else, it would have seemed tacky and garish, but Mr. Valentine wore it with a confidence that baffled Budd's mind. The man walked right up to Budd and snagged the cigarette from between his lips. He then stabbed out the ember on the bedside table.

"I'm here to kill Ripley Eagleson," he said. "And if you get in my way, I'll kill you too."

"We have captured the Blood Eagles. Reginald Pearce identified five of them, and we arrested them weeks ago."

Budd felt nauseous when Mr. Valentine laughed uproariously at his words. He moved to stand in front of the infamous outlaw and growled, "Maybe I'm still a little drowsy from my sleep being interrupted, but I don't get what's so funny."

"Reginal Pearce is Ripley Eagleson."

The End

Would you consider leaving a review on Amazon? I would appreciate it.

More westerns are in the works.